PRAISE FOR R~~~~~ ~~~~~~

**Raves for the Jaded Gentleman Novels**

*Obsession Wears Opals*
"Passion and adventure seamlessly blend as Bernard stirs a tale steeped in intrigue and secrets, keeping pages turning and interest high." –*RT BookReviews*

"Renee Bernard has redefined what makes a hero and heroine heroic..." –*Tina Ong, GoodReads*

*Passion Wears Pearls*
"Chemistry between the characters sparks and crackles with a vibrant energy that shivers up your spine keeping you on the edge of your seat well into the night." –*Veiled Secret Reviews*

"Renee Bernard hits another one out of the park!" –*Lindsey Ross, GoodReads*

*Ecstasy Wears Emeralds*
"Sensuality fills the pages." –*Publishers Weekly*

"Level of emotional force that makes sure you cannot put this book down!...Ms. Bernard skillfully weaves a tale of love and learning, friendship and betrayal to lead you down a merry path..."

*Seduction Wears Sapphires*

"An amazing read, I enjoyed it immensely...Ashe and Caroline are wonderful characters that made me fall in love with them from the beginning of the story." –*Night Owl Reviews*

"A fine book, well crafted, well researched, and an entertaining romantic novel...Historical romance fans will be delighted, I have no doubt." –*The Book Binge*

"What a refreshing new take on two people who from first sight are determined to detest each other...I was immediately engrossed with the fiery, witty dialogue and the curiosity of how this couple, who loathed each other upon their meeting, would come full circle to a beautifully shared love in the end." –*Ficion Vixen*

*Revenge Wears Rubies*

"Sensuality fairly steams from Bernard's writing. This luscious tale will enthrall you. Enjoy!" –Sabrina Jeffries, *New York Times* bestselling author

"If you're a fan of spicy hot romances mixed with a bit of intrigue and set in Victorian London, don't miss this one!" –*The Romance Dish*

"Galen's journey from emotional cripple to ability to love is captivating, erotic romance." –*Fresh Fiction*

**More praise for the "grand mistress of sensual, scorching romance"\***

"Sinfully sexy...Wickedly witty, sublimely sensual...Renee Bernard dazzles readers...Clever, sensual, and superb." –*Booklist*
   sensuality but a strong plotline and a cast of memorable characters. She's sure to find a place alongside Robin Schone, Pam Rosenthal, and Thea Devine." –*\*RT BookReviews*

"Very hot romance. Readers who enjoy an excellent, sizzling Victorian story are going to thoroughly enjoy this one." –*Romance Reviews Today*

"Shiverlicious! A captivating plot, charismatic characters, and sexy, tingle-worthy romance...Fantastic!" –*Joyfully Reviewed*

"Crowd-pleasing." –*Publishers Weekly*

"[This] steamy historical romance is [a] great debut for this new author...Filled with steamy and erotic scenes...The plot is solid and the ending holds many surprises...Tantalizing." –*Fresh Fiction*

# LADY TRIUMPHS

## FINAL BOOK IN THE BLACK ROSE TRILOGY

## RENEE BERNARD

*This book is dedicated to Pamela Clare because whenever I met you, you managed to inspire me with your grace and your laughter and I wanted you to know that even from afar, you continue to inspire me with your grace and now, with your courage. You probably don't even remember meeting me, but I will never forget meeting you. So this book is dedicated to you.*
*Just to you.*

*To win the bloodiest battle is to ensure that you have nothing left in your own veins first.*

— RAVEN WELLS

# CHAPTER 1

 ondon
1873

TIME BECAME the merciless tyrant that ground out the hours since Lady Serena Wellcott had fled Southgate Hall. The stunned and horrified look on Sir Phillip Warrick's face haunted her dreams at night and robbed her of peace even while she elegantly navigated her days.

Muted sounds of the London streets sifted up into the open windows of her drawing room and Serena did her best to listen to each element and ward off the melancholy that threatened to drown her. After all the years of priding herself on her self-control, this was no small battle. The founder and leader of the Black Rose was not a fragile school girl to lament the dark twists of a love affair gone wrong. But there was no more revenge to be extracted—not from Phillip Warrick.

She'd punished him enough. Finally. Utterly. It was enough.

If a part of her had expected him to chase after her, to catch her on the roadways to the city or to be on her doorstep before the sun set for one final vicious confrontation, Serena was in no mood to admit it. Instead, the days of denial had stretched out until it had been over a fortnight and he hadn't come.

*God help me, I wasn't truly ready to let him go.*

The weight of that one truth was crushing and wisely, Serena had never allowed it to come in an avalanche. Instead, it was a revelation she'd taken on with every new day, her raw intellect weighing it out like dark sand in a bucket until she could carry it without fear of it swallowing her whole. She sighed in acceptance of pragmatic wisdom. He hated her and now that she'd cruelly cut him with the one thing he'd never thought of—that there might have been a child from their time together years ago—he would truly never forgive her.

*Never.*

*Which might be far earlier than I am prepared to forgive myself.*

The taunt she'd thrown in his face would act like a festering poison in his heart until the only way to survive meant cutting her out of it. She'd intended to drive him off, to spare him from the dark entanglements of her life but...

She closed her eyes and allowed the bitter taste of irony to seep into her senses. To survive these last few years, she had transformed into a woman who derided weak sentiment only to suffer from the world's most common malady.

*This is ridiculous. The deed is done. Better he knows my true nature to recover and close the door on the past, once and for all. Was that not the aim of my last grand gesture? To free the man and let him stomp off? So why sit about pouting?*

A folded copy of the London Times slid off of her lap and she retrieved it from the floor. A small note in the social section recaptured her attention and Serena sighed. *What a midnight dark sliver of a cosmic jest! The Earl of Trent to arrive in London for the Season after years of refusing every invitation...*

*No more excuses. Nothing in my way. It is time.*

She pressed her fingertips against her temples to soothe the sharp pulse there. "I need to see the week's correspondence and begin to make a survey of the social season ahead. I need to make my plans."

"You need to eat." Pepper set down the lunch tray with a little more force than was needed, making the cups and tableware rattle.

"I'm not hungry, Pepper."

Pepper crossed her arms and began to tap her foot impatiently. "Oh, I'm sorry. I don't remember asking you if you had recovered your appetite, your ladyship. I'm fairly certain I did say that you needed to eat which didn't imply a question of any kind."

"You're not a very good bully, Prudence."

"Ha! I'm short in stature but I am mighty," Pepper said triumphantly as she lifted the silver cover over the plate. "So says Shakespeare, so eat."

"You read too much," Serena grumbled without any bite. Especially since she was the one who had insisted on Pepper's education and celebrated her friend's progress with her studies. "And I'm fairly sure that quoting the Bard to your employer is some kind of mutinous act."

"Oh, you've not tasted mutiny yet," Pepper continued to set out the meal as if there was no question of its consumption. "I've got that whole bit lined up in my head about 'movable feasts' and the like."

"I'm not hungry," she repeated uselessly.

"You've been nursing your wounds since we returned and I'd say it's been long enough. If you mean to die of starvation, then I suggest you choose another method. Something quicker, perhaps? Or less likely to cause the cook to rant from morning to night about all her wasted work and effort?"

"What a dear you are to think of it!" Serena smiled. "Send my compliments to Mrs. Holly and bring me my pistol."

"You, never!" Pepper squealed in protest and then caught the light of mischief in her mistress's eyes. "Oh, thank God! There. There you are, you wicked thing! Thank God in His Heaven!"

Serena dutifully picked up the fork. "I think every churchman in the British Empire just felt a chill slide down his spine at such a statement, Pepper. Imagine thanking the Lord Almighty for the likes of me?" She tasted the light crust of the meat pie and sighed, "Though I do love you more for the sentiment."

She set the meal aside and diverted to the small curved lady's desk against the wall, sitting to take up pen and paper. "I will commission Harriet for the season. Her reputation as an unforgiving chaperone is untouched."

Pepper picked up the plate and boldly brought it over to the desk. "As untouched as this lunch?"

Serena took another bite to make a gesture of compromise. "There. I am eating. Now, leave me to it."

"Hire the dragon after and I'll—" The bell at the front door rang and Pepper straightened. "I'll see to it."

"No need. Quinn will deal with any callers." The house had been closed to visitors since her return. The sound of a commotion in her front hall echoed up the stairs and both women exchanged questioning looks.

"Shall I—see if?" Pepper began but Serena waved her off, standing abruptly.

"Go. Take the tray."

"Are you sure?"

"Take it, Pepper. Go, now!"

Pepper rushed out with the entire tray, the service door closing behind her just as Sir Phillip Warrick burst into the room with Mr. Quinn, her butler, and two of her burliest footmen on his heels.

"Serena."

"Mr. Quinn," she addressed the butler calmly. "Let's leave the baron on his feet and let him have his say. I'll ring if I have need of you." Serena shifted back to offer Phillip the chair across from her. "Tea, Sir Warrick?"

Phillip shook his head in silent refusal waiting to speak until they were alone. "I didn't come for tea."

"No? What a shame! Mrs. Holly is an artist when it comes to a tea tray." She looked at him, expecting him to bark at the inane words or launch into some hateful rage, but instead there was an ache in his eyes that echoed the one in her heart. Phillip Warrick had not come for a fight. It was unexpected twist that robbed her of her wits. In every fantasy of his arrival, they had either murdered each other or floundered about in a dance of fire and ice to shatter the last of their hearts.

"You've lost weight." His gaze never faltered.

Her first instinct was to lie and say that she'd been ill. But there had already been too many lies between them. "After all my protestations, it seems I am human."

"Of all the things I have believed of you, I never doubted your humanity." Phillip ran splayed fingers through his hair, his nerves betrayed. "I've broken your heart. Again. Is that the only thing I am capable of as a man?"

"No." She kept her place, unwilling to risk touching him. "But I dared you to do it. Commanded you to do it, so I should be grateful for your obedience." A flash of useless vanity made her smooth back a curl from her face, mirroring his gesture. "If you came to gloat, I could spare you the effort but I completely grasp the need to balance the scales, so…" Serena took a deep breath and let it out, a proud queen facing her executioner. "Let's have the coup de grace."

"Serena," he whispered.

"Raven," she said. "I have just decided that I want you and you alone to call me Raven. I think it will give this conversation a poetic irony, wouldn't you agree?"

"I think the poetic irony of every conversation we have ever had is…above questioning." He closed his eyes, his countenance becoming calmer before he took the seat she had offered him. "Raven," he said, a man savoring the taste of a word on his tongue and her heart pounded at the realization that she was helpless when it came to him. He opened his eyes to look at her and began again. "Raven, is there a child?"

Tears threatened and her throat tightened in the painful grip of regret. "No. There never was." Her hands clutched the arms of her chair. "I was cruel. It was a desperate thing to say, to strike out against you."

"No child." He softly echoed her words, then shifted in his chair slightly. "But there *could* have been. I will curse myself for the rest of my days for missing it, for being so blind with my own anger and pain that I—I forfeited my soul and yours."

She tried to smile. "My soul is my own, you arrogant man, and I assure you it is well hidden in a vault somewhere. Mind your own."

"Raven, there may yet be a child. We were anything but careful at Southgate."

She gave him an arch look, unsure of where he was going with the conversation. "Phillip! Must we include a discussion of my monthly flow in this, already awkward conversation?"

"Yes."

"I am *not* with child."

"Then I can broach the next topic without delay." He gazed at her without any guile. "You don't make anything easy, do you?"

"It is not in my nature."

"I want you to tell me honestly what you think of me, Raven. What kind of man do you hold me to be?"

She shook her head. "I do not know."

"No? Am I a complete mystery to you?" he asked. "Am I a liar? Am I a villain?"

"No."

"Then what am I?"

"You are a good and honest man and a bit too trusting sometimes. If that is a fault, then I cannot say I would change it, even knowing what it has led to between us. I was once very trusting myself and I find that I like the quality in your character even if I have banished it from my own." Serena leaned forward. "I care for you—without needing reasons and my opinion of you is irrelevant if you've come to screech horrid things in my face, don't you think?"

He winced but held his ground. "I'm going to pretend that I've never done such a thing to inspire that notion and state that I have no intention of saying a single cruel word to you ever again if I can manage it."

"It's been a while since I left you at Southgate, Phillip. Your silence has been eloquent enough."

"I wasn't sure if you were up for a chase but that's not really all of it. I did start to rush after you to confront you before that carriage pulled away…"

"Did you?" she asked softly.

His eyes bore into hers, without pretext or guise. "I did but it started to rain and I had a strange moment that gave me pause. The tables were so completely turned and for once, I wanted to think before I acted. I wasn't sure if I caught you just then what I would say. Once again, I was so hurt, so angry, so lost. Even so, I composed a thousand ways to apologize for yet another incredible slight and then I wasn't sure if I had the right to any of it—to you, to happiness, to forgiveness. I allowed you to flee back to Town and have your escape." He continued quickly, recognizing the fiery spirit that awakened at the use of the word 'allowed' as her pale grey eyes sparked. "Raven, if you don't think that a single rider can outpace a four-in-hand, then we will have another debate on the subject later."

"Very well. You *allowed* me to get away."

"Only because if there was a punishment you needed to inflict then I deserved to sit with it for a while before I responded. I stayed at Southgate Hall to ensure that James was safely deported as you'd arranged and Delilah settled before…" He cleared his throat again. "Before I came for you."

"How is Mrs. Osborne? Is she faring well?" It was a ridiculous ploy to shift the conversation away from herself but she needed to catch her breath.

"She glows with happiness and seeing it, I came to understand how very miserable she must have been all along. How could I have missed the shadows that had overtaken my dear cousin?"

"Sometimes grievances and wounds come in small doses, accumulating over long cruel months and years and the change is so gradual that unless you are living it, you cannot see it." Serena smiled. "It is one of the rewards of my calling to see the transformation of a woman when she comes into her own."

"Raven." He shifted so that he was kneeling before her, his hips pressing against her legs to subtly part them, his supplication transitioning into an erotic position of hidden power. "I've come to you.

After everything, after all of it, I am here. I have begged forgiveness for that terrible day. I have repented every stupid moment of that last day and vowed to enslave myself to you and you alone in exchange for your forgiveness. You have shoved me into a creek, abused me at every turn, tortured me body and soul and left me in the rain and mud. I'm not sure what else is left. What else can I do? What additional proof of my devotion do you need?"

"For once, Sir Warrick, my mind draws a blank on the subject."

"You're infuriating, woman. Damn it, Raven. How can you be so calm? Tell me it is not every day that men are kneeling at your feet begging you for their lives."

She smiled. "No. Not *every* day."

"I'm an idiot." He stood slowly but lifted her up from her chair and into his arms. "But no more begging. Tell me there is hope and that we can yet find some way to craft a future together, you and I."

"You are not an idiot. I generally have no use for idiots, Phillip, but I—I find that I am very much in need of *you*. As illogical as that may be..." She shook her head. "I am not a woman who hopes. But I am a woman who needs."

He kissed her then without preamble, without pretense. It was a searing kiss that threatened to overwhelm them both with hunger and with relief at the passionate fires that still burned between them. Nothing had been lost. Phillip's kiss was commanding, lifting her up against him, tasting her mouth and ravishing her senses. There was no hint of begging or supplication now. He was the man who had always driven her desires and after nearly losing her, it was clear that Phillip Warrick was not going to relinquish the reins again.

"Oh, my!" she sighed as he finally released her. "Phillip, this is a dangerous devotion. Tell me you realize this."

"I love you, Raven Wells. I love you, Serena Wellcott. I love every incarnation of you, light and dark. It is all I can do. Am I overjoyed that you place yourself in harm's way to help others or that you trust at a glacial pace? No. Am I going to be prone to forbidding us to so much as play cards so that we can avoid any reference to someone winning or losing? Yes. Am I going to run at the first flash of those elegant claws? No. Never again. So name your terms, woman."

She took a deep breath. "I will not abandon the Black Rose."

He nodded. "So be it."

"I will never marry."

He didn't flinch. "We'll set aside that debate for another day. So long as I alone have you, for I will not share you with another man."

"If only you knew how truly selfish I have been with this heart, sir. Apparently once given, I lacked a single thread of human charity that would have compelled me to offer any other living soul a slice of it." She sighed. "Even when I hated you, Phillip Warrick, I was yours. Entirely yours."

"I will make no effort to reform you on that point."

Serena tipped her head to one side. "I assume *your* fidelity is also part of this arrangement?"

"Without question." He began to relax, the heat between them igniting again. "Anything else?"

"I am going to destroy Trent. It is time."

"Raven," he started to protest, the heat dying in an icy flare inside his chest. "Please, my darling. Let's let it go. The earl is the devil himself. Let Hell sort him out."

"No." She shook her head and pulled her hands away to stand. "My resources are in place. I have cooled my heels long enough to give him the illusion of my disinterest. I am going to destroy Trent, on my own terms and in my own way. And what I require is not your approval or complicity, but your strength to stand aside."

He came to his feet without effort. "To stand aside?"

"I will not ask for your help in this enterprise. There must be no hint of your involvement or he will sense it like a fox downwind of the hounds and I will lose him." She reached up to stroke his face, the soothing trail of her fingertips calming his brow. "My skills are unparalleled but even I cannot risk arousing his old obsessions when it comes to you, Phillip."

He shook his head. "I don't care what you claim. Your confidence

RENEE BERNARD

had to have suffered a blow at Southgate and these 'skills' that put you in harm's way will not shield you from Trent's madness."

"I'll make no inventory to you of recent lessons I've learned, Phillip." Her hands fisted at her hips. "I have named my terms, sir."

"He's more dangerous than you imagine."

"I know that even better than you."

Phillip shook his head. "What self-respecting gentleman could agree to this? What kind of man steps back and lets the woman he loves face a demon like that alone?"

"I won't be alone. I have the Black Rose and I have you to return to each night and to encourage me." Raven leaned in to kiss him softly. "Give me the greatest gift I could ask for, Phillip."

"And what gift is that?" He tasted the silk of her lips before she leaned back to look into his eyes. "My trust?"

Her eyes misted with emotion and at last, she gave them voice. "Revenge."

# CHAPTER 2

*P*hillip held his ground and studied her. The scent of her body and the jasmine perfume in her hair was already working against his intellect but he was determined to stay strong—at least long enough to navigate a conversation that would affect both their lives.

"I can't gift you with something you've proclaimed you'll have with or without me. I don't know if I can play the voyeur when every part of me is screaming that it is hardly the role of a gentleman to deliberately fold his arms while the woman he loves proposes to dance with the devil. It's not the role of any man." He gently reached out to grip her upper arms. "We have wrested our happiness from the maws of defeat. We could punish him by openly living happily ever after. What satisfaction can be gained from pushing for more? He's an eel of a man and not worth a minute of your time."

"Phillip. I will stop him. Not just because he betrayed my father's trust, used me so callously and destroyed the girl I was without a backward glance—but because I cannot in good conscience allow him the power to do it again. How many lives has he altered on a whim? How many souls have been crushed in his wake? How many more fates are twisted when his temper dictates imaginary insults or his inner demons demand more respect?" She held still in his hold, the strong emotional currents inside her anchoring her. "How many more Ravens will fall?"

"Are you to become the world's protector?"

She lifted her chin. "Not the world's but the women within reach of the Black Rose, yes. Yes, Phillip. I am Lady Serena Wellcott and I will not allow the Earl of Trent to shed the consequences of his cruelty. I will balance the scales and scrape the last of these scars from my soul or I will die trying."

"No. No dying, Raven."

She smiled. "As you wish."

"If I agreed to this…"

"Yes?"

"Then you would have to fully comprehend the implications. You jest but I have seen how lightly you value your life, Raven Wells. I have seen how careless you can be." He shook his head at the icy fear the memory of her bruised face evoked. "You would risk all to achieve your aims but that has to change. Because it is not your life alone you would sacrifice."

"Phillip—"

"There is no poetry in death, Raven. None. If you demand my solemn vow to support you in this cause without interference, then you have to know that if you fail, then linger at the golden gates, my dearest, for I'll join you before St. Peter has finished his first speech of welcome."

"You were ever the optimist, Phillip. But yes, I will ask the Devil to wait."

"Raven," he said, closing his eyes at the frustration that urged him to throttle her. "Swear that whatever revenge you need, the price won't be blood."

"His or mine?" she asked.

"Don't jest."

She shook her head. "I never jest about vengeance."

"Raven!"

Serena sighed. "Of course I will do my utmost to survive

unscathed. What sort of delightful revenge would it be if anyone other than Trent suffered? Besides I know Geoffrey Parke, the Earl of Trent, too well. He would never resort to violence, not directly. And the Black Rose is known for its elegant solutions and in this instance, I am aiming for perfection, Sir Warrick. Stop scowling at me."

"When I have agreed to this, you will never *ever* get to demand proof of my love and allegiance for as long as I live. Do you hear me?"

She nodded, a familiar wicked smile beginning to light her features. "Are those your terms?"

"Nearly. I have one last requirement."

"Let's have it."

"No more secrets."

Her gaze narrowed but then cleared as he watched her make the mental leap. "Yes."

"Yes?" he said warily. "That was…far simpler than I expected."

"Oh, I shall invent an elaborate ceremony where you lay prostrate at my feet and swear fealty to our secret society, something with incense and a foreboding amount of shadows and stained glass. What do you think?"

He nodded. "There should be a chalice, an obscene amount of candles and a sword if you're going for high drama. Naturally I will be looking forward to seeing what your costume of diaphanous black silk entails…or would that be too obvious?"

They both began to laugh and Phillip decided that he had had all a man could take of solemn vows and dark narrow escapes. Just as her balance shifted with their merriment, he bent over to sweep her up off her feet and lifted her into his arms.

"Phillip!"

"Where is the bedroom?"

"Oh!" Her laughter evaporated. "It's upstairs. Second floor. If you put me down, I will happily walk to spare you the effort of the climb with—"

He didn't wait for her to finish. Phillip was a man on a mission and he didn't care if she'd put her bed on the top floor of her home, or on a mountain top for that matter. He strode from the drawing room with his prize held against his chest, deliberately not looking at her too much to avoid the temptation to see to things on the nearest sofa or—

*Hell, I'll make love to you on the staircase, woman, and your staff can just recover their wits later.*

He surpassed the temptation by taking the stairs two at a time, winning her laughter at the playful betrayal of his impatience. She was light in his arms, an easy and welcome burden. She was also actively seeking to distract and tease him as he made his way through her house. Serena's hands roamed freely, loosening the buttons of his shirt front and caressing whatever skin she could bare given her position. The brazen gesture sent lightning arcs of fire through his frame because it heralded the change between them.

They were not cowering in the shadows.

Lady Serena Wellcott was mistress here and felt no need to disguise her desire for him from the servants. There was no pretense, no prevarication and for Phillip it was a revelation to taste how sweet life could be. He'd missed this. Their time together at Southgate had spoiled him. Once they'd overcome the worst hurdles of their past misunderstanding, they'd enjoyed their secret trysts without reservation and once behind closed doors, without shame between them. Serena was a fearless lover and so generous and yielding, it took his breath away. To regain her trust, there was nothing Phillip wouldn't contemplate.

To have her back in his arms was a fierce joy that almost unmanned him. He'd been a given a rare second chance at love and he was not going to squander it ever again.

*Even if this joy only exists within the confines of this house—for now.*

He quashed the distracting notion, returning his complete attention to Serena in his arms.

"Which door?" he asked, his voice rough.

"There. Large one directly at the end of the hall," she purred. "Shall I walk the last bit and allow you to catch your breath?"

He smiled wickedly and shook his head. "You think me winded? Poor woman." He stepped to the door and then rather than juggle with the door handle or risk loosening his grip on the precious bundle in his arms, Phillip kicked the door open with the authority of a pirate.

She squeaked in surprise but her expression betrayed nothing but delight at the aggressive move. "Phillip. Kindly break no more hardware. Mr. Quinn will have fits."

"You can comfort him later." Phillip kicked the door closed with equal force, earning another glowing look from Serena.

"Yes. Later."

He set her down only when he'd nearly reached the large four poster bed set against the room's far wall. He took no notice of the room's décor and knew that if quizzed, he couldn't name a single color in drapery or artifacts beyond the burgundy russet ruched bedding that made up his primary goal. He was not there for a civil tour of her private chambers.

And Serena wasn't offering him one.

He pulled her into his arms to kiss her, unwilling to end the connection between them even as they undressed in a mutual rush, each giving the other just enough assistance to achieve their aims, wickedly caressing the flesh beneath layers, teasing sighs and groans with every fumbled tie or lost button.

Phillip Warrick was many things, but he conceded that a lady's maid wasn't one of them as he wrestled with an inordinate amount of layers upon layers that made up a fashionable day dress and its underpinnings.

Even so, within minutes, he'd dispensed with every barrier and bared her body to his. They were not strangers to each other but the moment of rediscovery always had a power all its own. He drank in the sight of her, a study in contrasts with her coloring but also the firm ripe curves and lean lines that enslaved him body and soul. She'd truly lost weight, but retained her attractiveness in his eyes. She would reacquire her softness and it pleased him to think of it. If anything, the undeniable evidence that no matter how proudly she tried to announce her independence, her appetite said otherwise. He smiled and pulled his mouth lightly across her bare shoulder.

*Without me, she would waste away... She mourned for us and missed me more than she would ever say—and there is no small part of me that wants to crow to know it! Never again, Serena.*

Serena groaned when his next kiss lifted her up off her feet again, adding to the insatiable craving that whipped through her body. The friction of her body across his and the glorious press of his stiffening cock against her belly wanted her to cry out, to scream in sweet frustration. She wanted his hands, his mouth, his cock, everywhere at once in an illogical storm of lust. It made no sense. She had gone years without him but now accepted that she had barely survived a single fortnight.

*It is ridiculous.*

*I don't care.*

*If love has finally made me ridiculous, then so be it. I'll recover my pride later. For now, I will have this!*

Serena pushed away from him, desperate for control but also to savor him. Her fingers reached out to grip his arousal, her touch instantly changing him, adding to the heat of his body and the sensation that he was increasingly carved in marble sheathed with the velvet of his skin. His breath pulled quickly through his teeth, and she smiled at the beautiful sound of his struggles to rein in his needs. Serena, however, was not in the mood for restraint of any kind. She traced the pulse of his blood as it flowed through him, resting kisses on pulse points or anywhere the thrum and beat of heart betrayed his excitement. If his breath caught in his throat, she would mercilessly pursue his pleasure with her mouth and her hands, until Serena was confident that she alone was the mistress of his satisfaction.

With a wicked smile, she slid down onto her knees without releasing her grip, and then without hesitation, left him in no doubt of her intentions. She kissed the ripe swollen plum-sized tip of his penis, lavishing him with the stroke of her tongue then took him deep into the warm pocket of her mouth, no teasing preambles were necessary as she allowed desire to dictate her actions. Her hand followed the slick path of her lip as she lifted and lowered onto his flesh, moving in a symphony of admiration and erotic torture. It was an act of worship, a pagan rhythmic dance unselfishly chasing only his fulfillment.

Phillip's only choice was to keep one hand on the corner post of the bed for balance and then to surrender to her, to all of it. Because he couldn't think beyond what she was doing to him—and he didn't think he could have recited his own name at that moment.

She brought him to the brink and then leaned back, teasing him with her breath only, looking up at him with a sweet hunger that threatened to push him over the edge. It was indescribable to see Raven Wells on her knees, her breasts grazing his thighs, her mouth hovering over his cock and the wicked gleam in her eyes.

"My God, I think I might have a heart attack…"

"A complaint?" she asked softly.

"No! Who the hell complains if—"

Her mouth encased his throbbing flesh and Phillip instantly forfeited speech. This time she was relentless, the speed and magic of her strokes and kisses plundering his will. He climaxed in a shuddering series of rocketing implosions that robbed him of breath and reason. Every romantic plan was forgotten, every intention to torture her slowly and see to the gentlemanly code that dictated that is was 'ladies first' when it came to pleasure.

"H-holy….hell…" His knees buckled a bit and Serena stood to push him down onto the bed.

"I should apologize, Sir Warrick but I…had worked up a terrible appetite for you these last few days and…" She sighed, a blushing and extremely unapologetic woman who happily straddled his belly. "I seem to have a weakness for this version of you."

"Which version is this?" he asked, his brain beginning to unfog.

"The one where you kick in my bedroom door."

"Ah," Phillip said wryly. "I'm going to keep that in mind, Raven."

"I will warn Mr. Quinn to be prepared for all future repairs." Serena wiggled her hips slightly, attempting to carefully avoid his oversensitive flesh.

Phillip's body had a very different reaction to her shift, stiffening without warning and catching them both off guard.

"Oh, my!" she exclaimed cheerfully.

Phillip lifted her off of him, pressing her down into the soft bedding and covering her with his body to part her thighs. "Seeing as how I have already breeched the door for now, Lady Wellcott, what say we make the most of the day?"

She nodded, eyes wide. "Yes. I say, yes."


AFTERWARD, they lay in a lazy tangle and watched the beams of sunlight lengthen across the room to herald the end of the day. They'd pursued pleasure until they were both sated and happily sore from their efforts. Even so, Serena waited for the inevitable return to the topic at hand.

"So, about Trent, have you already made plans then?" he asked her in the quiet of the room, her fingers lazily making trails through the rough curls on his chest.

"No. And I don't want to talk about Trent. Not now." She sighed. "Once the game starts, it will be soon enough for him to dominate my thoughts and fill my days. I don't want to invite him into these moments."

"What a wise woman," he said softly and rewarded her with a kiss. "Now let's discuss how I'm to get around this chaperone of yours..."

# CHAPTER 3

*S*erena sat back against the blue velvet upholstered seat of her closed carriage and made a quick internal inventory. A member of the Black Rose had sent word that the Earl of Trent had accepted an invitation to one of the Season's inaugural events and from there, Serena had wasted no time in gathering the information she needed. She had made no open inquiries to anyone outside of her secret networks, preferring to camouflage her interests to guard them from casual gossip. The women of the Black Rose, and more often their servants, had provided all the details she needed.

The earl rarely bothered with Town, and generally only came into London briefly for business or for his own benefit or when politics required his presence. Like many, he preferred his own stomping grounds in the country or the limited company of his investment cronies.

But this season just as the papers had reported, he would be in London for the duration. It was impossible not to appreciate the timing of Providence and the twists of Fate that put her in a position to move against him at last. With Phillip Warrick at her back, there was nothing in her way and no one to stop her.

Though for all of Phillip's ardent vows to cooperate, Serena smiled at the memory of his pacing about like a bear in her bedroom that morning as she'd prepared to go out. She might have indulged him in a passionate distraction to settle his nerves but the clock was an unforgiving mistress.

As the carriage halted in front an elegant home at the center of a tree filled square, Serena settled her thoughts on the afternoon ahead and the start of a dangerous game, perhaps the most deadly game she had ever played.

No matter what Phillip had said, she did not underestimate Geoffrey Parke. Even on the surface, he was an enemy that provided no simple solutions. The earl's business interests were good and his estates profitable. He had no weakness for gambling or whoring, nor any other vice that would expose him to social ostracism. He was yet unmarried but had no requirement of a direct heir since he possessed a nephew somewhere that she had never met.

At first glance, he was untouchable.

But Lady Serena Wellcott was not given to impulse or impatience and she was determined to look as long as it took until she found a chink in his armor. She already knew that Trent was an imbalanced soul and that his greatest weakness was his ego. One look at Phillip reminded her of the lengths he would go to if his "male pride" was wounded and she highly doubted that time had lessened his mania.

But pride wasn't exactly a straight path leading to a man's downfall…

"Lady Wellcott, you are as prompt as ever." Lady Harriet Lylesforth gracefully swept forward to meet her on the steps. "Though I am not pleased at the notion of your arriving alone! What if I had been delayed?"

"Harriet, unless someone has deployed a garrison to fight you in the streets, how is such a mishap possible?" Serena kissed her friend on both cheeks then leaned back to admire her new ensemble. "You are a force, Lady Lylesforth, and may I say, a little too pretty when you wear dark grey in the middle of the afternoon."

"Do not make your Dragon blush!" Harriet admonished. "It is unseemly!"

Serena nodded, surrendering with a smile and taking her friend's arm to climb the stairs to Norwich's grand home. If there were any authority on what was "seemly" it was Lady Lylesforth, and no one in all of Great Britain wasn't aware of it. All of twenty-eight years old, she would have been considered far too young and too beautiful to take on the role of a forbidding chaperone, but Harriet was not a woman to be defined by her age. Famous for her rigid standards and sharp tongue, Harriet was a widowed woman with a tragic past and she was renowned for her inviolate and uncompromising character.

Only Serena knew her secrets and their friendship was forged in the strange fires of the Black Rose and the loyalty of shared combat.

Harriet would be her chaperone or "Dragon" as Serena had affectionately dubbed her for the season and ensure that not a breath of gossip could mar Lady Serena Wellcott's path in the weeks ahead.

"Have most of the guests already arrived?" Serena asked.

"All that matter," Harriet said. "I have spoken to Lady Norwich and she is giddy to see you out so it's a soft landing."

"Good."

"Lady Wellcott! You bring the sun with you and enlighten our little gathering in every way possible!" Lord Norwich said as he crossed the foyer to greet her. "When my wife revealed that you were to join our party, I abandoned all pretext of hating garden parties then and there!"

"I loathe the draft of the outdoors and hope you've provided cover if the weather changes quickly, Lord Norwich," Harriet said archly, forcing Serena to stifle a giggle.

*Oh, she is going to press this to the hilt! What fun!*

"Lady Lylesforth! I would never risk anyone's delicate health by failing to do so! But what a pleasure to see you as well. What a... delight." The man's enthusiasm dimmed as he bore the brunt of Lady Lylesforth's unfriendly attention. "Though I am saddened to see you still have not completely abandoned your widow's plumage, dear lady."

The furious spark in her Harriet's eyes was sharp enough to cut diamonds. "Her Majesty has yet to abandon hers, Lord Norwich. I felt at liberty to make a similar choice and did not think to suffer comment."

"Oh, no. I...meant..." Lord Norwich glanced at Serena with an open plea for mercy in his gaze. "Aren't you both lovely!"

"Harriet has agreed to be my companion this season," Serena explained.

"Naturally," Lord Norwich replied, a lifetime of manners intervening to save him. "How very sensible of you, Lady Wellcott!"

"Thank you, your lordship. I was so happy to receive your invitation. You and your wife have been so kind to include me. But how is your Emily?"

"She grew up, Lady Wellcott! When I wasn't looking and may I say, without my consent!"

"No! She is a child yet and there is time to enjoy her sweet company!" Serena protested mildly, completely aware that poor Lord Norwich was the father of a sixteen year old on the brink of breaking quite a few male hearts. Like most daughters, the first heart in danger would be the father who adored her and who would be forced to loosen his grip when she was launched into society.

"Her company is not so sweet at the moment," he sighed then smiled. "She has likened our care to that of an ogre holding her in a tower but—what parent would do less? One more year to hold her back and then...she is as eager as a colt in the traces."

Serena took his arm, patting his shoulder in a comforting but useless gesture. "Next season, she can run her first race and you will see. You will watch her with pride and understand that no one can take a father's place, sir, and," she lowered her voice conspiratorially, "after paying for a debut trousseau and all those dancing slippers, you may be of a different mind when a suitable young man raises his hand."

Lord Norwich laughed. "You always know what to say to cheer me, Lady Wellcott!"

Harriet shook her head. "We should go in and pay our regards to your wife, Lord Norwich. We have monopolized your time enough."

He ducked his head meekly and waved them through the main

doors to show them into the party. Then it was the usual social blur of familiar faces and new introductions as Serena mapped out the battle-field and allowed Harriet to keep them moving. Norwich's garden party was early in the season but an elite gathering thanks to Lady Norwich's close friendship to Princess Louise.

Serena took a slow turn around the gardens, stopping to greet acquaintances as needed but making sure that she did not stray too far into the gathering's center. She wished to keep a close watch out for Lord Trent's arrival but also ensure that if he spotted her it was not with the impression that she was being shoved under his nose.

It wasn't a long wait. Harriet squeezed her elbow and then subtly shifted away to leave Serena alone, heading toward the refreshments.

Lord Trent's arrival was a simple thing without fanfare or fuss but for Serena, it was as if the wind stopped and the birds fell from the trees. There he was. Familiar and nearly unchanged after seven years, impeccably dressed in an afternoon suit with the polish of a gentleman as comfortable in a royal court as he would be in a brothel. He'd been her guardian since she was ten and until she'd left to elope with Phillip Warrick, Geoffrey Parke had held a special place in her affections. Lord Trent had played the role of a kind, wealthy uncle and if Phillip hadn't shoved Trent's letter into her hands before throwing her out of that carriage, Geoffrey Parke was the man she would have unwittingly returned to for comfort and care.

A slithering ache of dread moved down her spine at the memory and the certain knowledge that but for that letter, Lord Trent's rejec-tion would probably have been the final push she needed to end her own life.

*But I ended it differently, didn't I?*

*Come, Serena. Think of oaks and sunshine and Phillip's kisses because if Trent sees a single phantom in your face, then we lose before we start.*

He spotted her, his expression one of delighted surprise as he came toward her. "Lady Wellcott! My goodness, what an incredible stroke of luck to meet you at last!"

She smiled, holding out her hands to him and walking forward to close the gap more quickly. "And the best kind of surprise! Lord Trent! You are unchanged and as handsome as ever!"

"Am I? Men do like to see themselves as carved in stone and immune to time but—I cannot fumble with a similar claim about you for I swear, you have done nothing but blossom!" He kissed her on both cheeks then stepped back to assess his forgotten ward. "I was a fool and underestimated how beautiful you would become, Lady Wellcott."

She shook her head. "It was that first startling impression of a child with knobby knees sharp enough to blind the most discerning man that misled you sir."

He laughed. "Brava!" He leaned in to add, "I knew you would land on your feet but I never dreamt you would do so with such grace. I am so pleased and—awestruck, *Lady Wellcott*. Well done."

She curtsied and treated him to a wicked and flirtatious wink. "It was ever my desire to make you proud, sir. And yes, you are clever to perceive that I do not answer to my old name."

His reaction was so openly appreciative that she nearly gasped at it. His gaze dropped to admire her décolletage, the color in his face heightening.

*Are you...interested, sir? What an unexpected twist...*

"What a delight you are, Lady Wellcott!" he said, the gleam in his eyes was unmistakable.

She smiled, forcing herself to warm to the words. "Are you in London for long, Lord Trent? Will this be my only chance to see you out and about?"

"You will scarce believe it but I am here for the season. I took a grand little house near Hyde Park on Long Street and have determined to prove that I can still hold my own in the cruel cold of a London summer."

Serena shook her head. "I cannot credit it. You hate the city, I remember you saying it a thousand times."

"I still do," he admitted with a sigh. "But now that I see you, I have forgotten why."

"Oh! Such flattery and now I know you are only speaking kindly because of a gentle nod to nostalgia." She risked a pout, determined to assess what kind of threat he posed. "Of course, what am I doing fawning all over my dear former guardian and greeting you with smiles? I should have stomped on your toes for my troubles with Warrick but the sight of you drove it from my mind!"

"Nonsense! I knew that boy wouldn't get the better of you." Geoffrey's cheerful countenance never wavered. "But if you insist on punishing a man's toes, then I'll have to ask you to dance when the opportunity arises. You may march on my instep to your heart's contentment—and then we can be friends again."

"A happy solution!" she conceded brightly.

"Here, take a turn about the garden with me, Lady Wellcott." He held out his arm and she took it, gracefully falling in step next to him. "Nostalgia is a wicked thing, in my opinion. It is the gilded lies we tell ourselves when the truth doesn't suit."

"I have always enjoyed the truth. Perhaps that is your influence, Lord Trent."

"Rightly so!" He straightened his shoulders proudly. "Did I not aim to create the perfect woman? And there you stand, as beautiful as a goddess, unflinching and without silly sentiment to cloud those eyes!"

"Taking all the credit, are you?" she teased him.

"Naturally." He grinned. "Though to see you now, I regret the waste of such a pretty bit of bait for so sluggish a fish as Warrick."

She playfully struck him lightly on the shoulder. "Do not say his name. I had nearly forgotten the fool yet it's twice we've invoked him so let's not risk a third just in case some pagan god of mischief sets out to ruin our day by plunking him in our path."

"I missed your wit." He shook his head. "It was worth every penny I spent on your education, Lady Wellcott."

"I wonder why you would bother to educate me if all I was ever meant to be was a pretty little piece of bait?"

"Why?" Geoffrey was nonplussed. "Why not is a better question. I never paid much attention. As you yourself said once, I instructed your tutors to cover the very basics to ensure your appeal and then the rest..." He shrugged his shoulders. "I just wished you to be happily occupied and out of my hair."

"How fortunate for me!"

"Yes, a nice windfall," he agreed easily. "I knew it couldn't hurt. Some of the best courtesans were quite literate."

"I was to be a well-educated whore?" It took every ounce of her skills to laugh with the question and soften its edge.

"Oh! That is a harsh comparison, Lady Wellcott! I apologize! I knew you would rise above it all if you had the means and perhaps a part of me hoped that keen wit of yours would triumph to reign over us all."

"No need to apologize." Ice coursed through her veins as she lightly pressed herself against his arm. "I'm flattered you trusted my instincts."

"What flattery? A good intellect can defeat anything short of a bullet, in my humble opinion." He grinned as merrily as a man on his birthday. "Tell me. The Duke of Northland's been polite but distant since he reacquired you. It was the abrupt end of his correspondence that alerted me to the possibilities that you had solved the puzzle of your parentage and wisely attached yourself to him."

"It seemed practical to seek him out."

"When did you realize that the duke was your father?"

She shrugged with a dismissive sigh. "It was a vague guess that served me well. You were so careful to hide his letters whenever I came into your study and then your pet name for me made me wonder."

"Pet name?" his brow furrowed as his memory failed to produce the detail. "What pet name was that?"

"Duchess."

"Ah!" He laughed merrily. "Too clever! You are too clever, Lady Wellcott!"

"All right, Lord Trent. Tell me the truth, since we have both confessed to loathing anything less. Why are you in London for the season?"

He smiled. "There's that persistent curiosity that betrays that underneath it all how very feminine you are! Very well, if you must know, I am here for my own selfish interests. My nephew, Sir Adam Tillman of Yorkshire, is to come to London before the week is out and I promised my sister I would be on hand."

"That doesn't sound very selfish."

"It is! This is the boy who stands to take my place at Oakwell Manor along with the title. I've seen little of him, well, nothing of him as my sister's health is eternally poor and she's insisted on keeping her boy close. But he's a man full grown and enough is enough! I intend to inspect my heir apparent and see what the future holds."

Serena laughed. "Do you mean, to see what you can make of the future?"

"Ha! Perhaps!" Trent shamelessly reveled in the insinuation. "A man must do what he can to protect his legacy in this world."

"Only a fool would do less," Serena said. "Well, I will admit that I am simply glad for any excuse that brings you out. It has been too long."

"We will be at Lord Drake's soiree on Saturday next." He stopped to face her, his expression earnest. "Come and dance with me, Lady Wellcott. Meet my sausage fingered nephew and make me smile. Give me a glimmer of hope that the weeks ahead hold more than the humorless efforts I was going to make proving that I could live forever just to spite my sister."

She laughed. "That is a great deal for me to promise, but I will say yes to the dance and then let's see." Serena touched the rim of her bonnet to adjust it to better flatter her features and Lady Lylesforth interrupted them on cue holding two crystal glasses of punch.

"Lady Wellcott! I should not have to hunt you down and may suspect you claimed to be parched only to..." Harriet gave the earl a dismissive look. "To fall prey to unguarded conversation."

"Have you met the earl, Harriet? This is Lord Trent. Lord Trent, may I introduce the unredoubted Lady Lylesforth."

"Charmed." Geoffrey bowed his head a nearly invisible inch. "Surely this is not *the* famous Widow of Stone? You are too short and too pretty to be the very same, madam."

"It is a ridiculous nickname but regardless of its application, I fail to see how my height or appearance should affect my credibility—or cause you such astonishment." Harriet gave him her iciest look. "Perhaps we should make introductions another time when you are feeling less giddy."

The earl cheerfully ignored her censure. "I remember something about Lord Lylesforth but the details of his demise escape my memory...Two or three years ago, yes? Something gruesome, wasn't it? All my sympathy to you, dear lady, for your tragic loss."

Harriet's spine stiffened. "How sensitive of you to bring it all up—and in one go! But at least, he comes to mind whereas you, sir, are someone I know nothing of and have heard even less." She set down the two glasses of punch abandoning them to signal the women's pending withdrawal. "I never trust men who fail to create a name for themselves."

Geoffrey smiled. "I do love a woman with a sharp tongue. Remind me to introduce you to my nephew when he arrives in London. The boy could use a bit of toughening up."

Serena watched the exchange with fascination as Harriet was unfazed by Trent's barbed wit. She adored her friend's strength and knew it was not a show. As for the earl, Serena knew it was a different story and that he was only testing and pushing because her chaperone had pricked his pride.

"May I note that your nephew may also need a good lesson in manners if you have been his mentor, your lordship? Come, Lady Wellcott. There is an acquaintance of note that we should pay our respects toward and I see no reason to delay."

*And that round goes to Harriet!*

Serena smiled. "Of course, Lady Lylesforth." She gave Trent an apologetic nod. "Until Lord Drake's then, your lordship."

"I look forward to it with vast anticipation, Lady Wellcott!" Trent said with a theatrical bow. "Yes, until then!"

She sailed off with her chaperone, her head held high.

"My dislike of the male species is reconfirmed," Lady Lylesforth stated. "Was that as you wished regarding Lord Trent?"

"It was. Is there a water closet or…a quiet room I can use?"

"Of course." Lady Lylesforth directed her to a well-appointed room on the ground floor and left her in privacy.

Serena locked the door behind her, leaning against the carved oak to catch her breath.

*Was that as I wished?*

*Oh, God.*

She barely made it to the basin before retching up the contents of her stomach, mercilessly sick until she was so weak she feared might not be able to walk. She pressed cold fingers against her forehead and waited.

*I have quite literally agreed to dance with the Devil.*

She heaved again at the thought, and finally gave in to shock and tears.

The game had officially begun.

# CHAPTER 4

"*W*as it a lovely outing, your ladyship?" Pepper asked cautiously. "Sir Warrick insisted on awaiting your return."

"It was." Serena answered and then looked to Phillip who was leaning against the mantel in the drawing room. "Not—lovely but a bit more of a success than I'd expected our first time in."

Phillip raised one of his eyebrows, patiently waiting. "But he was there."

Pepper withdrew and Serena held her breath, taking her place on the settee.

"He was there." The words hung in the air between them.

"You'd said he would be." Phillip crossed over to sit across from her, his expression full of concern. "Was he cruel?"

Serena shook her head. "In a strange way, yes, but by all conventional measures, I should say not. He was…thrilled to see me, delighted at the reunion and oblivious to any harm he caused. It was—almost more cruel to be so regarded but I fully comprehend my value to him all those years ago."

"And what was that?"

She lifted her shoulders lightly and dropped them with a small sigh. "I'm confident that I held a place at least one step over one of his horses but I may not have surpassed those swans he tried to add to the pond when I was thirteen." Her expression sobered with concentration. "He was obsessed with those birds if I recall it rightly."

"Raven."

She waved away the memory and the look of sympathy in his eyes. "Phillip, the point is not lamenting the man's lack of paternal affections. The point is that I have learned more of his mind. He recalls my life at Oakwell Manor with vague attention and my part in your "downfall" with pride. But he is blind to me as a threat and has no notion of any trespass." She sat up a little straighter, a woman in command. "He has essentially become you."

"Me?"

"Well, you as you were seven years ago. How is that for delicious irony?"

Phillip shook his head. "I don't perceive where any of this is delicious and I do not acknowledge any resemblance!"

"Then I withdraw the comment. I meant only to allude to the twist that Geoffrey Parke is oblivious to any danger and believes that everyone around him is a friend. Or at least, so overconfident of his powers that he cannot see how one slight woman could present a threat." Serena stood to stretch her legs and pace to help her thoughts fall into place. "It is Trent's turn to play the lamb."

"Raven, you cannot think he'll let you put a ribbon and a bell on his neck and dance him into the slaughterhouse. He won't *play* anything."

"You have no taste for revenge, Sir Warrick. Trust me. All men dance once you discover the melody that pleases them."

"Pity that," he said sarcastically then gave her an apologetic nod. "Very well. I am a novice. What next, mistress?"

"I am to attend Drake's ball next week. Lord Trent has expressed a desire to dance with me."

"Like hell!" Phillip leaned back in his chair. "May I say for posterity's sake that I loathe this plan already?"

"Your objections are noted." She paced to the windows to look out.

"He admires me because he believes himself to be my maker like Pygmalion. I am his Galatea." She touched the glass, allowing the cool glass to temper the heat in her fingertips. "It is perfect."

"Perfect?"

"I am his Creation. Who better to author his destruction than a creature of his own design? I know him. I know his male pride and enormous vanity. I know how to make him laugh, to draw him out and push him."

"Push him where?"

"I don't know yet. But he is facing a critical turning point. He has clung to bachelorhood the way a child clings to its mother but without offspring, a nephew stands to one day inherit his title and holdings." Her pacing picked up speed. "The nephew is coming to London and Trent is to host him."

"Poor boy," Phillip added.

"I know Trent. He'll want to influence and remake him if he can, into some version of himself that appeals to his vanity. But if the boy falls short, it will be hard for him not to turn against him. Heir or no, I don't think the earl's pride will allow a lesser man to attempt to fill his shoes—much less walk the halls of Oakwell Manor as its master."

"He has no choice, Raven. If the boy stands to inherit, it hardly matters what Trent thinks of him." Phillip stretched out his legs, settling in to admire the quick turns of her mind. "He might be irritated but that's not exactly world shattering."

"We'll see. Remember that your idea of a minor infraction and the earl's notion of vast injustice are two different things. I will meet his nephew and make my own judgment but my instincts say that if he is a sliver of the disaster I am praying he is, then I may need to do very little." Serena returned to her chair. "The details will come but one thing is certain."

"I am almost afraid to ask."

She smiled. "I am going to need a new ballgown and dancing slippers."

"I want to be the one to take you dancing, damn it."

She shook her head. "I will not be seen with you publicly until this matter is finished. Stop pouting."

"I am most decidedly not pouting."

"Then go downstairs please and wait for me to change for dinner. We'll have a quiet meal together and if you are charming, who knows where the evening may lead?"

He sighed but a wicked heat came into his eyes. "It will inevitably lead to me sneaking out the back alley from this house but I am willing to see if I cannot be diverted from departing for a few hours yet."

She stood to place her palms against the thrumming pulse of his heart. "Phillip. A more charming approach would be to see if *you* can divert *me*—not the other way around."

"I do see the wisdom of your perspective."

He kissed her possessively, his mastery thrilling her as Phillip demonstrated that he knew exactly how to please her best. She opened her mouth quickly to taste him, welcoming the velvet touch of his tongue to hers. His kisses gave rise to a renewed hunger, a heat that she didn't wish to cool. Serena clung to him, shivering at the delicious sensation of her bones melting away.

"Dinner," she whispered.

Phillip lifted his head, the cloud of desire fogging his own vision. "I'm not hungry."

Serena smiled, savoring the sweet power that held them both in thrall. "Well, I am. I didn't get so much as a cucumber sandwich and if I'm to have my strength for the evening ahead..." She reached up, caressing his face. "Go. Wait downstairs and let me change for dinner. Please."

He sighed. "I do love the way you say please."

"I suspect I will repeat that word quite a few times before the sun rises, Phillip."

"I'll take that as a promise."

Serena balanced up onto her toes to steal one more quick kiss. "I am a woman of my word, my love."

ALONE UPSTAIRS with Pepper to change for dinner, Serena held as still as she could while her hem was repaired. She looked down at her friend, a pang of affection making her smile. "I don't think Sir Warrick will be looking at my feet, Pepper. Would you like to let it go?"

Pepper looked up at her in shock. "Are you mad? Allow *my* Lady to touch one tread of that staircase looking one thread short of perfection? Where's your pride, woman?"

Serena shook her head. "A momentary insanity must have seized me."

"I'll say!" Pepper teased, clucking her tongue in mock disapproval. "Now's not the time to be dropping standards!"

The jest struck home and Serena lifted her head, her smile fading. "You're right. Now is not the time to…soften."

"Don't start fretting up there."

"I am not fretting!" Serena put her hands on her hips but mastered herself before stomping her foot. "Seeing the earl has—this game will go quickly, Pepper. If I'm to outwit him, there is no room for doubt or hesitation."

"You'll get him in the end," Pepper said then bit through the thread to finish it off. "There!" Pepper stood, her petite stature making it an uneven proposition but Pepper addressed her as an equal. "He rattled you today."

Serena nodded. "I—I was sick with it."

"Just so," Pepper whispered. "A belly full of hatred is not an easy thing to digest."

"I'm going to destroy him, Pepper." Serena said. "But I have a feeling that I have never had before and it frightens me."

"Say it."

"All the ugly revenge I have dealt out like so many cards, but this time, I am too close. Planning vengeance is like planning a murder, isn't it? Except this won't be like knife work where the cut is made and all you have to do is mind your petticoats to step around the blood puddles. This time I think it's going to be like a bomb going off and if it's to work, then I'll be looking in Trent's eyes when the explosion comes."

Pepper shuddered then smiled. "I shall go to Hell for getting such a thrill when you talk like this. You, who haven't so much as squashed an ant, but I swear you make my blood go cold."

"They are metaphors, Prudence."

"I know! Though what a glorious thing that would be if you put a bit of dynamite under his chair..."

"Pepper!" Serena chided and then started to laugh. "It *would* be a simpler and somewhat satisfying scenario."

"Here, let's get your hair set." Pepper pulled out the vanity chair and Serena settled in as her hair was braided and pinned atop her head. "As we're on the topic, I'm to meet with Mrs. Fitzherbert's maid tomorrow on her afternoon off. She's on the same square as the house the earl has let and I'm to get a full report from her."

"Brilliant."

"It's Sir Warrick's that got you twisted up over all this but don't you let go of that man's hand." Pepper's fingers never slowed. "You're not saying it but that's why you're afraid. It's a messy business and even with what he knows after witnessing your handiwork to help his cousin, you're worried he hasn't seen you at your worst."

"Perhaps."

"He loves you. That won't change. But if you turn from your own will, you'll never forgive him for it. Right or wrong, makes no difference. You're too stubborn and set to it, your ladyship."

"I'm not turning away from anything."

Pepper nodded and said no more.

Serena looked at her reflection, drifting back to the problem at hand. *It would be a miracle if Phillip's devotion truly holds through this. She's right. I'm fearful of losing him if I go too far.*

*But Fate doesn't bend to sentimentality.*

*The circle is closing fast and I can nearly see the shape of it. The surprise is how familiar all this ground seems. I can hear myself at seventeen saying that I would sacrifice anything and everything to be happy. And here comes the test at last.*

*What will I risk to end the Earl of Trent?*

*What wouldn't I risk?*

The answer never came and she accepted that nothing was off the table.

Not even her own happiness.

# CHAPTER 5

$S$erena made a quarter turn, noting the way the detailed ruching in the bustle drew the eye down, accenting her narrow waist and figure. "Madame Montellier! It is a wonder. But are you sure the fashion is so…elaborate this season?"

"It cannot have too many layers in the cascade, your ladyship. The latest dictates of Paris do not overtake English sensibilities, but a balance must be struck. Do you not agree?"

Serena nodded, smiling at the delicate politics of a woman's skirts. "We must hold our own, Madame Montellier, and make a statement of our own."

"For the Empire!" The dressmaker proclaimed with a mischievous gleam in her eyes. "And to make every man in London swoon at the impact when you walk away, Lady Wellcott."

"It is not every man I hope to affect," Serena demurred. "Perhaps just one."

Pauline Montellier's expression instantly transformed into rapt surprise at the admission. "Is it true?"

Serena shifted to face her. "We'll see. When I come back to retrieve my purchases and in the Season ahead, I hope I can rely on you to once again discreetly convey what news I give you."

The dressmaker nodded eagerly. "Gossip is the easiest currency to spend in London, Lady Wellcott. And one that I am grateful you accept in return for my debt to the Black—"

"Madame Montellier," Serena said, cutting her off gently. "I am only happy to see your shop thriving and my favorite dressmaker with roses in her cheeks."

Pauline blushed as if on cue. "Was there anything else you required today, Lady Wellcott?"

"I will need several ensembles for the weeks ahead. I wish to make this a Season to remember."

Serena stepped down from the dais, accepted assistance back into her own clothes and then they began to quickly shift through the fashion plates, before Pauline retrieved her sketchbook to modify designs as her best customer dictated. Madame Montellier was completely familiar with Serena's style and with the lightning fast speed of her selections. Where other women dithered over lace for hours, Lady Wellcott could specify every detail of an entire, flawless trousseau in minutes.

Pauline's breath caught in her throat as a fortune was committed in silk and labor. "Why do I bother with other clients when I have your generous patronage, Lady Wellcott?"

Serena laughed, then patted her friend's hand. "Because without a shop with such delightful clients, however will you spread the gossip that I need you to share?"

Pauline nodded. "My shop is yours."

"No. Yours, dearest, all yours but I do need use of my room today, Madame."

"Yes." Pauline reached into the deep pocket hidden in the folds of her skirt. "I have the key here in anticipation of your appointment." She held out a heavy ornate key tied with a black silk ribbon. "If you would allow me the liberty of lighting a few coals, Lady Wellcott. That room is so rarely used and I wish you to be more comfortable."

"You are kind, Madame, and a true friend. But I will be quick and have no wish to trouble you." Serena took the key and waited until the modiste had left before walking over to the fitting room's back wall and pulling aside the brocade curtain that hid a locked door. She opened it smoothly and then locked the door behind her. She found the lantern on the table and lit it quickly, her familiarity with the space making her movements smooth and efficient in the darkness. It was a small square windowless room decorated sparsely enough to pass but it served its purpose. Here in the back of fashionable dressmaker's shop, the Black Rose could meet secretly with anyone without risk of any association with her house or her person.

Beyond the dress shop's uses for spreading strategic gossip, Serena had required use of this windowless room as the price to Madame Montellier when Pauline had asked the Black Rose for aid. Pauline had been one of her very first members and of all the assets Serena possessed, her tiny secret room was one of her most prized. The key to this room conveniently also opened the door to a narrow alleyway next to the dress shop and gave her a discreet portal to London and London to the Black Rose. She could meet anyone here without discovery and without question. After all, women were expected to spend hours at their dressmakers so if her carriage waited on a public street outside of Madame Montellier's establishment, not an eyebrow would be raised.

And who would ever suspect the proper Lady Wellcott to have private conferences with criminal elements, sordid characters and unsavory persons in some sort of secret sitting room in a dress shop?

Inside the room, the outer door was disguised with a heavy brocade curtain to shield any light that might escape if it were opened at night. Serena drew back the thick cloth, unlocked the portal and then had to throw the bolt open to finally achieve access for her guests. She'd insisted on the additional security to both keep her friend's shop secure but also to guarantee that no one could stumble into her hidden parlor from the outside world.

On the steps outside, two large brutish men as identical as buttons awaited her. "Gentlemen, I do love you for your promptness."

"We take pride in it, Lady Wellcott," Jack said after they'd stepped inside through the curtain and bolted the door

"A man's not worth his salt if he can't keep his appointments," Jasper echoed.

Physically, they were so intimidating, it made her smile. Broad and strong, the twins were walking mountains of muscles with faces that appeared carved from granite. It was an asset they'd never fully utilized until she'd discovered them as unsuccessful players after a failed theatre company's demise. The men were reduced to guarding stage doors and clearing pub brawls. She'd hired them both and was pleased to be their sole and extremely generous employer. If a mark needed intimidation, the twins earned their keep. Their acting skills and looks extended beautifully to the role of "brutish killers" but in reality, she knew the boys wouldn't kill a spider if it strolled across their breakfast table.

"Are you both well, gentlemen? How is your mother faring these days?" she asked.

"She is much better since the weather's improved," Jack said. "Her doctor is very pleased."

"And she loves the new house," Jasper added. "She swears that no countess lives better!"

Serena shook her head. "She is blessed to have two such devoted sons. Don't forget to set aside wages for yourselves as well. You are kind to see to her but even your mother would wish to see you preparing for your futures. If you're each to marry one day…"

The twins blushed. "We're hoarding every shilling for—well, for such a hope."

"Good." She hovered over them like a meddling aunt, but she liked the role. "Now, onto business!"

"If you pardon, your ladyship," Jack interrupted her. "May we ask?"

"Yes?"

Jasper cleared his throat. "H-how is Pepper?"

"Pepper?" she asked in feigned surprise.

"She didn't seem herself and we've worried in the days since," Jasper said.

"When she came with your last packet after your return to

London, she was too pale." Jack crossed his arms. "Too quiet! We asked but she pushed it off."

Jasper nodded. "Something's not right though. Barely a smile for us."

The twins had a soft spot for her beloved friend and she knew it was extremely mutual. Serena eyed them both briefly, acknowledging silently that she trusted them both to their marrow and that if ever a young lady deserved and needed two devoted strong guardians, it might be Prudence. "I will tell you this only in complete confidence. There was a bit of trouble in the country. She was…nearly overtaken in an attack by our host, a Mr. James Osborne."

"He's dead!" Both men spoke at precisely the same moment in frightening synchronicity.

She held up her hands, palms outward to calm them. For once, she believed there was no theatre involved in this show of fury. "I have dealt with him, gentlemen. Surely you know me well enough by now to know that I would never allow such a trespass to go unpunished?"

"Punished is not dead," Jack said grimly.

"Dead is dead," Jasper said.

She gave them each a slow smile. "Trust me. You could not have done better. He will never recover and never trouble another girl again. *Never.*" Serena stepped closer to them, lowering her voice. "I said she was *nearly* overtaken, sirs. It was a frightening experience and no doubt, has made her spirit temporarily cautious. If you wish to be her champions, then I would advise you to do it with compliments, kind words and patience. She already likes you both but she would be mortified to think that you saw her as wounded or damaged in some unspeakable way. Women struggle with shame even when it isn't warranted. So just be sweet! And see if you cannot earn a smile or two, yes?"

The muscle in Jack's cheeks tightened, betraying that he was gritting his teeth. "She has *nothing* to be ashamed of! Pepper is the dearest thing and that animal had no right to make her think less of herself when—"

Jasper touched his brother's shoulder. "We'll see it right. Pepper *is* the dearest thing and she'll come back around to realize it."

Jack nodded, his stance relaxing at his brother's touch. "Yes. We'll see to it. Compliments and kind words. That we can do easily enough."

"And patience," Jasper added with a smile. "That might be a little harder."

"Patience," Jack repeated softly, his eyes locked onto his brother's gaze. "For Pepper, we will put the mountains to shame with a show of it."

The twins turned back to her, better prepared to focus on the business of the day. Jasper nodded. "What do you need of us, Lady Wellcott?"

Serena lit another lamp and the three of them settled in to review the recent workings of the Black Rose. While she'd been gone, the twins had made sure that no loose ends unraveled and that any active marks of the Black Rose were not presenting any surprises. Payments were collected and discreetly distributed per Serena's instructions. She shared what details she could of her plans and the importance of the upcoming weeks. Serena required a smooth Season and for all conduits of information to be open and clear, so the generosity of the Black Rose would be palpable.

"Trent's address in London," she handed Jack a folded note. "Fitzherbert is his neighbor so quietly make sure that every servant in that house and if possible on that street is happy to help, gentlemen."

"God, Fitzherbert's cook makes those ginger pies! Remember them, Jasper?"

Jasper smiled. "We nearly drowned in those pies after Your Ladyship intervened for their girl! I went from feeling like a happy hero to wishing I'd never tasted pie."

Serena laughed. "Serves you right for eating two dozen in one sitting!"

Jack shrugged sheepishly. "We didn't want to hurt anyone's feelings, Your Ladyship. And it was…our first time…you know…playing the good guys."

Jasper nodded. "That was a change, wasn't it?"

Serena stood and the men followed suit, their meeting coming to an end. "You are always the heroes, gentlemen. Never forget it."

Jack elbowed his twin in the ribs. "Who needs pies when you can make grown men piss their pants just by looking at them, eh, brother?"

Jasper elbowed his mirror image back, their humor catching. "Truer words have never been uttered by an idiot."

"Gentlemen!" Serena stepped back. "I will see you in a few days."

They nodded sheepishly and without another word, retreated through the hidden door into the alleyway. Serena locked the door behind them, and carefully made sure that no sign of their meeting remained. She extinguished the lantern and then made her way back to the empty dressing room.

She pulled the bell and Pauline came quickly to discreetly collect the key.

"Are you sure you wouldn't prefer to keep it yourself, Lady Wellcott?"

Serena shook her head. "It is safe with you and I only use the room during hours of commerce."

Serena smoothed her skirts and returned to the front of the store as she began her retreat from the shop only to run into Lady Hodge-Clarence.

"Lady Wellcott! What a thrilling chance! I did not realize that you patronized Madame Montellier's tiny shop. I thought myself a genius to have discovered her and a wicked woman to keep her all to myself." The dowager's admission was less an honest confession than a subtle pout at the notion of competition.

Serena ignored the complaint and kissed the woman on both cheeks. "Ursula, every woman who knows you seeks to follow in your footsteps. Why would I be any different?"

"Ah, true. It is a burden I must bear with grace." Lady Hodge-Clarence sighed dramatically. "If only I could get them all to march in step, wouldn't that be something?"

"It would certainly be a terrifying enough sight to win the day for workhouse reformation. Parliament would weep in horror and give your ladies committee all that it wished, Lady Hodge-Clarence."

"You are an angel to say it, Lady Wellcott!" The dowager stepped back. "I shall call on you for support before our next club meeting. I am expecting your continued support."

"You have it. Always." Serena said.

"Madame Montellier! My schedule is overrun and I am too pressed for time. See that we do not dawdle for this fitting!" Ursula barked at the dressmaker before smiling at Serena. "The Season has just started and I am already awash in commitments."

"From your elegant demeanor, one would never guess at it," Serena commented praying that Ursula's wit was too dull to notice the sarcastic edge in her words. "But I shall leave you to your fitting and beg forgiveness for envying your gowns when I see you out and about, Lady Hodge-Clarence."

"Ridiculous flattery coming from you, Lady Wellcott!" Ursula said but the color in her cheeks and her girlish smiles betrayed that the words had done their work. "So very kind of you."

"I shall leave you to it," Serena nodded and stepped back but not before Ursula shifted back to Pauline.

"I want nothing you've made for anyone else, Madame Montellier! Do you hear me?" The dowager swept from the showroom toward the private fitting rooms.

Serena didn't flinch at the change in the woman's tone, but gave her friend a sympathetic look when the dowager's back was turned. It was the way of the world, but it was not the way of Serena's world. Dismissed, she left Pauline to manage her next client.

*Ursula is a selfish cow but she'll serve a purpose one day. Even if it's just to salaciously repeat a bit of gossip I've manufactured, or confirm my reputation as a conservative and charitable woman... but that doesn't mean I don't long to slap her walrus whiskered face.*

# CHAPTER 6

The day of Drake's ball unfolded in rare glorious sunshine and Serena had ordered every window in the house opened to take in the fresh air. She sat at her desk to attend to her correspondence and did her best not to be distracted as Phillip paced the room.

"We should take the carriage out for a ride through the park," he suggested. "It's too fine a day to be a prisoner, Raven."

She smiled and set down her pen to turn toward him. "What a wretched jailer I am! I release you from this dungeon. Go for a ride if you wish, Phillip, but I am not about to destroy my schemes with an impulsive and public ride in an open carriage through Hyde Park with Sir Phillip Warrick at my side. Word would reach Trent before he sits down for tea."

Phillip rewarded her with a surly and searing look. "When this is over, woman, fair warning that I intend to impulsively and publicly make it clear for all to see in an open carriage that I am the man at your side and in your bed."

"What a scandalous notion!" she exclaimed, her cheeks warming with approval. "I do love it when you threaten to be wicked, Sir Warrick."

"I'll do more than threaten. Set those letters aside."

She laughed, shaking her head. "Patience, my love." She retrieved a note from the top of a small stack to show him. "According to Fitzherbert's maid, the earl is a quiet enough neighbor and has received few calls. He's gone out to meet his business cronies at his club but no one else."

"How in the world does Fitzherbert's maid know where the Earl of Trent is going or who he is meeting?" Phillip took a seat next to the desk.

"Apparently the dear girl has taken a keen interest in the earl's driver and the man is proving to be very talkative." Serena answered him without looking up from the paper. "As most men are after a bit of exercise."

"Raven! Tell me you do not have this girl prostituting herself for—information about Trent!"

Serena looked up startled. "Don't be ridiculous! Phillip Warrick! Don't make me throw a paperweight at your head!" She placed the note face down on the desk's surface. "That woman's natural proclivities are her own to manage and if they serve my purposes, then I'm grateful for it, but she was rogering the earl's man before I made my first inquiry. It's luck, pure and simple, so cease that scowling."

"I apologize."

"I'll consider forgiving you later." Serena crumpled the small note and threw it at him, forcing him to smile. "Behave, Warrick!"

He retrieved the ball and handed it back to her contritely. "Has his nephew arrived?"

"No," Serena said. "Apparently not. I'd thought to meet him tonight but we'll have to wait and see."

"I pity the poor boy with Trent as an uncle. What twisted little soul comes from that family tree?" Phillip leaned back in his chair, a new idea seizing him and he gifted her with a wicked look. "Has *anyone* seen the boy? God, why do I have this sudden hope that he's a club-footed hunchback?"

"Stop trying to make me laugh." Serena shook her head. "I am sure he is hale, hearty and whole. And we should probably stop referring to him as if he is nine and in short pants. Trent said he is a grown man so it hardly suits."

"Yes, but it gives me immense pleasure to imagine him as some squat crippled hedgehog so I hardly care."

"I won't spoil your fun then."

"Raven," Phillip sat up, his demeanor changing. "I have agreed not to interfere but I cannot simply sit idle or I'll go mad. Give me something to do. I don't care if it's assisting you with your correspondence and overseeing your calendar to make sure you don't miss a single opportunity to murder Trent."

Serena rolled her eyes but sighed. "I'm not going to murder him."

"Let's not make any promises you can't keep," he said with a wry grin. "Employ me, Lady Wellcott."

"You would make a horribly distracting social secretary, Sir Warrick."

"Should we discuss my wages?"

She stood to shift until her skirts were pressing against his legs, parting his knees. "Your wage would surely be commensurate with your skills. Are you well-skilled, Sir Warrick?"

"To date I have not received any complaints, your ladyship."

He drew his palms upward around her waist and across her ribcage, then up to skim the rich curves of her body, as Serena bent over him, her lips lowering to graze his with the softest fires of her touch. If she'd meant to simply tease him with the game, it was clear that all bets were off.

"Kiss me like that and I'll never complain about being banished from your side in public again."

"What a temptation, sir!" She released him gently. "Please, get out and enjoy the day. Take a ride in the park and stretch your legs. Go home and make sure your servants haven't reported you for missing."

"Very well. A ride and I will put in an appearance at my town home but I make no promises to stay away for long."

"I would never wish for that."

Phillip smiled. "There's a relief."

SUNSHINE BECKONED and a rare fresh breeze that made London perfumed and alluring won over his objections. He set out for a ride into Hyde Park, anxious to make the most of the day and find his balance. Phillip had never flourished in confinement and it felt good to ride out, even if it involved slipping from the stables to take a narrow brick lane from Lady Wellcott's property to avoid any prying eyes. The clandestine nature of their relationship was an unpleasantly familiar wrinkle and he was doing his best not to be distracted by it. After all, he'd spent years longing for a happy resolution and for some relief from his guilt and loss. Chafing at the slight imperfections of their arrangement didn't seem like a wise course but it occurred to him that not once had they ever enjoyed an open courtship or public connection.

At least this time he could take comfort that it may be a temporary issue. Once she'd dealt with Trent, Phillip was confident that her fears would ease and he could renew negotiations for a more traditional relationship. But failing all else, he was wise enough to acknowledge the social storms to be weathered once the Ton got wind of Lady Serena Wellcott's sinful choice to acquire a lover without a thought of marriage. He doubted she had thought of the price if she lost her social standing. Her current and future schemes all relied heavily on her ability to move about unhindered.

*Then again, I may be spending the rest of my life as her secret.*

His brow furrowed as the notion settled uncomfortably against his heart. If his Cousin Delilah safely delivered a son, his family would likely relax their scrutiny and lighten the pressure for him to marry and produce an heir. He could play the bachelor and clandestine role of the Black Rose's consort without interference. But after years of wearing the mantle of his title and role as head of the family, a part of him regretted yielding the chance to make Raven his wife and lady. His imagination began to weave the picture of a babe in her arms and the life they could still have if she surrendered to—

"Mind yourself, man!"

Phillip reined his horse in sharply to avoid the collision with a carriage. The park was naturally crowded thanks to the weather and his daydreaming had nearly caused a ridiculous accident. Shame at his lapse made his face burn and his expression was grim. "I am terribly sorry."

The male passenger in the open carriage was not in a gracious or forgiving mood as he needlessly pulled the woman at his side protectively into his arms. "The reins are in your hands, sir! I suggest you use them!"

Phillip touched the brim of his hat, bowed, then spurred his mount on to leave the scene. He was mortified at the mishap, disgusted that his thoughts could become so entangled that he had nearly steered his horse directly into a barouche.

*I know that love can make a man blind but I've never heard an instance where he forgot how to function entirely!*

Phillip grimaced. "The reins are in my hands. God, there's a message from Providence itself!"

*What am I doing?*

Phillip guided his horse off the path and halted under the shade of a large oak tree to gather his thoughts. He took a deep breath and looked out at the parade of well-appointed carriages and riders out enjoying the day. With new eyes, he studied the lovers and friends, the social games and formal greetings. He watched the show and players as they moved across the stage and waited for reason.

*I'm too far in to turn now. It seems foolish to worry about what the future holds with Raven when it's the present that stands in our way. She's set on destroying Trent and I cannot blame her. Hell, I hate the man as much or more than she does! But my instinct is to avoid him, to forget him, to cut him out and just get on with our lives...*

Thinking of Trent made everything painful, tainting his memories and spoiling clarity. The temptation to end Trent was potent but there was also an appeal to trying to lure her away from all of it, to kidnapping her for a luxurious stay in Paris until she was so deliriously happy that there was no room left for the past.

Both ideas were overturned.

He'd asked her for her terms and she had stated them. He'd accepted them without a breath of protest, determined to prove that he was a man of his word, a man of honor and the one man she could finally rely on.

God help him, he loved her.

Raven was like an inviolate force of nature that he didn't fully comprehend, but what man needed to understand a deadly storm to appreciate its beauty and power?

Raven was the dark center of his world.

It was impossible not to admire her keen intellect and talent for inspiring loyalty. He'd barely caught a glimpse of the tip of the iceberg that comprised her invisible empire, but he suspected it was vast. He enjoyed the new privilege of being in her confidence and holding her trust.

Not to mention the renewed pleasures of her bed.

It may not be the marriage he'd long ago envisioned, but then nothing in his life was the way he'd envisioned it. So why would Raven be any different?

Pride was a hard thing to smother and Phillip was wise enough to recognize the source of his anxieties. The answer finally became clear because any inkling of a life without her made every protest instantly stop.

She had asked him to stand aside and he had promised to keep out of Trent's path. Phillip tipped his head back, looking up at the sunlight through the filter of the oak's broad leaves. "It would be easier if I weren't acquainted with your suicidal nature, Raven Wells."

*I will not lose you again.*

*Not even to one of your own dangerous schemes.*

*I will keep my word. I'll stay out of the way but that doesn't mean I'm going to sit around my club, drink brandies and whistle in the dark.*

He was a grown man and a free citizen of the British Empire, not a prisoner in the maven of the Black Rose's lair. The love of his life had already proclaimed that she had no use for fools.

And so Phillip was determined not to act like one.

And if he felt like stretching his legs tonight and attending a ball...

There was no one to stop him.

# CHAPTER 7

*S*erena arrived at the ball with Lady Lylesforth who had conceded to the evening her dark widow's plumage only by the barest degree. Harriet wore dark purple threaded with black velvet trim but Serena knew better than to compliment her on the change. Her chaperone's expression was a mask of defensive ice.

*I could not have chosen a better woman to play chaperone in all the known world. Bless her. Harriet can wring tears from a Cossack if she's in a mood.*

As they ascended the stairs into the house, Serena was confident that her own appearance would hold its own. The dress she'd chosen was a masterpiece in a vibrant sapphire blue with an underskirt of gold. The décolletage was modest but cut to reveal the top of her shoulders and the fine shape of her figure. Only when she walked away did the daring display reveal itself as the bodice was cut to show off her beautiful upper back. The gold filigree choker at her throat was accented with three fine gold chains of varying lengths tipped in sapphires that cascaded down her spine.

They'd arrived late enough to ensure that the party was well underway and the orchestra tuned for dancing. Serena made a demure turn about the room, greeting a few acquaintances and making note of more than one man in the grand salon who had suffered at the hands of the Black Rose—not that they knew it. Most of her victims never suspected a woman's interference in their troubles. Those who knew of Lady Serena Wellcott's hand in their misery were in no position to betray her, so she walked with absolute confidence amidst her peers, with ally and victim alike.

She had a healthy respect for her enemies but no fear. Life had taught her that it was only the enemy you couldn't name that held any power. And tonight, she knew her enemy's name.

Geoffrey Parke, Lord Trent.

She felt far stronger facing him this time, convinced that it was the impact of seeing him after so many years that had given the man the edge at the garden party. The theory was tested very quickly when the earl approached the women, his usual smile firmly in place.

*Definitely better. Thank God I need not worry about getting sick on the man's shoes...*

"Lady Wellcott." The earl took her gloved hand to kiss it. "The night was crawling by until this moment. I'd begun to worry that you were going to renege on that promised dance."

"I never forget my promises." She resisted the urge to yank her fingers from his. "You remember Lady Lylesforth, of course?"

Lord Trent released her hand and nodded at Harriet. "How could I forget? Though who would have recognized you in such a festive color, Lady Lylesforth! So daring!" His voice dripped with sarcasm, the jibe at her dark wardrobe unhidden. "And such a relief! You are too young to play the widow, your ladyship."

"I do not *play* at being a widow, Lord Trent. My husband is dead. I should think that fact pays no regard to one's age." Harriet skillfully opened her fan with a sharp flick of her wrist. "What a pleasure to meet you again and have my first impressions reinforced. I do admire a man who is consistent in his character. Come away, Lady Wellcott."

Serena stepped forward to touch the earl's arm lightly. "Lord Trent! Make amends this instant or that will be that and you will forfeit that dance and a Season beyond."

Geoffrey managed a fleeting pout. "I must be losing my touch but I apologize, Lady Lylesforth. You may wear any color you wish and not have your beauty diminished in any way. I was a boorish clod to try to tease you out of your delightfully dour disposition."

Harriet glanced at her Serena before yielding. "Apology accepted."

Serena had to bite the inside of her lip to keep from laughing as Geoffrey slowly realized that Harriet was not about to seal her forgiveness with anything even remotely resembling a smile.

At last, he cleared his throat and simply directed his attention to what he perceived as a friendlier quadrant. "The Drakes appear to have invited all of London. I've never understood the impulse to over-crowd a ballroom and declare everyone's discomfort the price to pay for the company."

"Not even to show off one's popularity and ability to overcrowd a ballroom?" Serena countered.

"Oh, well, there is that." He smiled. "Come, let's see about that waltz if only to satisfy your honor, Lady Wellcott." Trent held out his arm and she took it with Lady Lylesforth's tacit permission, politely allowing him to escort her toward the grand ballroom.

The room was draped in green bunting to create a festive spring like theme. Candles gleamed and every polished and mirrored surface added to the glittering effect. They took their place on the dance floor and the music began.

Serena smiled, feigning a shy glow combined with a lively awed interest in the swirling masses around them to avoid having to look up into the man's face endlessly. The earl was not a polished dancer and after their second minor collision with another couple, Serena intervened to spare his pride.

"I see your wisdom in complaining about the lack of restraint in Drake's invitation counts. Would you forgive me if I asked for a breath of fresh air, your lordship?"

"Not at all. Let's see if we cannot escape the throng and find a drink without your chaperone fainting in shock."

They made their way to one of the salons, arranged for the over-flow of partygoers, the din of "private" conversations making Serena smile. "Ah, yes. This is much better." It wasn't a striking improvement but at least she'd eliminated the risk to her toes and the disgusting contact of Trent's hands on her person.

"God, I'll have lost Adam completely in this madhouse."

"Is your nephew here then?" she asked with genuine surprise.

"Yes. He arrived just this afternoon and I insisted on dragging him out. He couldn't miss tonight."

"Just for tonight's affair?" She glanced about the room. "It is one social occasion in a string of them unless I have missed its significance."

"You have. You are missing the notion that you are here and that I had the opportunity to demonstrate to my nephew that the most beautiful woman in London was cheerfully in my arms." He lifted his chin. "I am yet a man to be reckoned with."

"You are indeed."

"Ah! There he is!" Trent upheld one hand to wave over his nephew and Serena turned with interest to see what kind of man would one day become the next Earl of Trent.

A fat man huffed toward them and she forced a smile to her face only to feel the world take a strange sidestep when the man diverted toward the punch bowl. Serena's brow furrowed in confusion until an entirely different man emerged from the crowd and she struggled to make sense of it. She politely held her ground, waiting for another more likely candidate to step forward but when the man's path didn't waver toward them, she accepted the new twist.

"Uncle. It is awkward enough to stumble about this house without you hailing me like a hackney," he said calmly only to stop mid-stride as his eyes met hers.

Serena blinked.

"Lady Serena Wellcott, may I present my nephew, Sir Adam Tillman of Yorkshire? Adam, Lady Wellcott is the daughter of a dear friend of mine and…well, as you see, an incomparable beauty."

Serena nodded as Sir Tillman made an awkward half-bow, openly unsure of the protocol. She took the opportunity to gather her composure and prayed that Trent hadn't noticed the lapse. Because Sir Adam Tillman was *not* nine years old, *not* squat like a hedgehog or misshapen and *not* sausage fingered. He was at least six feet in height, broad shouldered and lean, so ruggedly handsome she nearly giggled at the strange humor of providence. Only a year or two past his thirtieth year by her best guess, he was a male specimen in his prime gloriously appealing in the way he artlessly held his ground. Pale hair the color of ripened wheat streaked with gold betrayed that he was not a man to bother with combs and pomade. His skin was unfashionably bronzed and eyes the color of a summer sky openly assessed her in return.

"Lady Wellcroft…it is a pleasure to meet you."

"Wellcott." Trent corrected him mercilessly. "Dear God, man."

The muscle in Adam's cheek jumped as he clenched his jaw tighter and the blue in his eyes darkened and Serena instantly knew more of him than any speech could convey. He was not enamored of his uncle or enthralled by the earl's notorious charms. And by Trent's vague introduction of her, it was clear that her old guardian wasn't giving his heir any history lessons. "Forgive me, Lady Wellcott. I was— distracted in the moment."

Serena smiled and gently waved away the apology. "I am surprised you could hear the introduction at all in this terrible din, and I am not so easily offended."

"A ruddy faced brute, is he not?" Trent asked. "I still suspect my sister of packing up one of her footmen to throw me off the scent…" The earl shrugged. "What? Look at him! He looks like a Viking warrior trapped in an evening suit! Or even worse, I swear he smacks of an American cowboy!"

Her composure deserted her for a moment and she gasped at the open insult, bristling in Sir Tillman's defense. But Adam cleared his throat, then gave his uncle a look of absolute nonchalance.

"Your wit betrays you, uncle. For by those words, one would infer that you expect all the men in our family to be weak, pale skinned doughy wastrels so you could recognize the resemblance."

Trent's eyes widened before he grinned. "My! There's a flash of fun! What do you think, Lady Wellcott?"

Serena's breath caught in her throat. "I think you must tread carefully, Lord Trent. It doesn't seem wise to provoke a man so well-armed."

"Yes, I like him, too," Trent conceded. "Even if he has wasted most of his life apparently trudging about in the elements like an itinerant carpenter building bridges and whatnot." Trent clapped his nephew on the shoulder. "No worries, Adam! Plenty to do at Oakwell Manor when your time comes, eh? You can design and build fancies to your heart's content."

Adam winced but then nodded. "I'll keep my worries to myself, Uncle Geoffrey. No fear." He shifted his attention back to Serena. "Would you care to dance, Lady Wellcott?"

"I would be honored, Sir Tillman." Serena smiled and then noticed the flash of disapproval in Trent's eyes. "No fear, Lord Trent. I'll return him with his toes intact in just a few minutes."

Adam led her away before the earl could summon a protest and Serena savored the escape as he escorted her back toward the main ballroom where the orchestra was in the midst of a reel. As they waited for the next dance, Serena seized the opportunity for a more private conversation.

"Did I hear the earl correctly? You build bridges, Sir Tillman?" she asked.

He nodded. "Yes. I am scandalously in trade and hold a professional degree as an engineer and architect. My uncle is very disappointed in me."

Serena smiled at the dry delivery and gleam of defiant humor in his eyes. "Lord Trent is disappointed in anyone who doesn't need his approval."

He looked down at her, openly pleased. "And you, Lady Wellcott? You do not think less of me for dirtying my hands?"

"I like and respect you more for it. This room has enough useless men in it who cannot button their own coats, don't you think? If they growl at you, it is only because they are envious and you make them look lazy in comparison." She glanced out over the crowded gathering. "When they are gone, the world will be unchanged. But who knows what monuments an architect and engineer can create as his legacy?"

"Dear God," he sighed, and she instantly pivoted to see if she'd overstepped.

"You think less of me for speaking my mind?" she asked.

He shook his head firmly. "No. Not at all. I was just...amazed and exhaustion has muted my manners." He straightened his shoulders. "I should thank you for the pledge to keep my toes safe, madam, but I have to risk looking ungallant if I point out that I am not as confident that I can make a similar promise," he said as he surveyed the milling crowd. "I am fighting to stay atop my own feet after the grueling journey to London and cursing my pride for allowing my uncle to poke me into proving that I was up for any adventure tonight. You are in danger, Lady Wellcott."

"Oh," she said, then went on. "In my experience, danger is largely missing from a woman's confined and restricted existence. I believe we invented dancing for the excuse to put ourselves into the fray. Besides, until you have danced the quatrain with a certain Colonel Marcus Bellicorte you have never tasted terror—so I think I'm up for the challenge."

"You give the remarkable impression that you are up to any challenge, madam."

"I suppose I am. Although if you see Colonel Bellicorte marching toward me, do not be disappointed if you see me making a hasty retreat."

He laughed, a deep bass melody that surprised them both. "God, I can't remember the last time I laughed!"

"Then I am glad for it," she said. "With Lord Trent as your uncle, you will need a good sense of humor to hold your own. But here, the test comes. Have no fear, sir. If your strength fails you, I can faint with the theatricality of a dowager and spare your pride, your toes and your reputation."

"You are my champion, Lady Wellcott."

The music ended and the transition of dancers departing the floor interrupted their conversation. At last, he led her out and they took their place near the center of the room in a small pocket of space. She politely placed her hand in his and entered the formal frame of his arms for the waltz. He was an inch or two taller than Phillip, but something in her rebelled against the impulse to make any further comparisons.

*Concentrate, woman. He is neither friend nor foe, and even if he appears to be an ally, his loyalties will fall where his fortunes lie.*

"Lord Trent should never have forced you out," she noted. "But I suspect it is a compliment."

"A compliment?"

"If he can outlast a man decades younger than he is, he shall preen over it for the rest of the Season." Serena risked candor. "He is no doubt attempting to demonstrate his strength and may see this as his only chance to do so and win. Unless you plan on criss-crossing England continuously in between putting in social appearances?"

He shook his head, replying even as he skillfully protected her from traffic. "I'll avoid the roads for a while and thwart him by getting a good night's sleep. My uncle's machinations are a good introduction to the subtle workings of his mind. I suspect, he is a man used to getting his own way."

She smiled. "A terrible habit you are going to break him of in the weeks ahead."

"That is a good guess." He looked down into her eyes and Serena had to bite the inside of her cheek to remind herself to focus her attention on her feet and not on the alluring power of his gaze. "Lady Wellcott, after meeting you, I may have to reconsider my position against insipid social gatherings."

"Oh, my! Just upon one meeting?" Heat flooded her face and she prayed it wasn't too obvious. "Sir Tillman, no matter how clever or entertaining I prove, I cannot counteract the dull tedious hours of London society. Though perhaps the distraction of all those mothers shoving their daughters in your path may add to the enterprise?"

He laughed again. "Hardly!"

"Don't underestimate them, Sir Tillman. The cunning of a scheming mother inspired by a future earl who has the audacity to appear without a wife?" She lowered her voice conspiratorially. "You must be on your guard."

"My mother must have given me a similar warning at some point but are you offering to protect me, Lady Wellcott?"

"Without weaponry?" she asked in mock horror. "They'll tear me to pieces!"

"I shall keep a wary eye out then, and do my best to endure alone; or protect you if a mob begins to form." He pulled her closer only to spare her a lumbering collision from a nearby gentleman who was openly fighting to keep a rein on his overly enthusiastic dance partner. "I have you, Lady Wellcott."

She was sure he'd meant it innocently enough as an assurance but her throat tightened as the sensation of his embrace and protective care encircled her. "You are too kind."

"Is it too forward to ask, Lady Wellcott, if there is a Lord Wellcott? I meant to say, are you married, Lady Wellcott?"

She shook her head. "No." Serena kept her face averted from his as if the confession were awkward for her. "There is no denying the truth. I have never been married and have no prospects nor designs in that direction, which places me firmly and happily on the precipice of irrevocable spinsterhood. You are safe, Sir Tillman." She lifted her head to look him squarely in the eye. "I am not a threat to your bachelorhood."

Movement across the room caught her gaze and she realized that Trent was on the edge of the crowded ballroom watching their every move.

*Is that jealousy I detect? Oh, my. Could it really be this easy?*

She looked back at Adam, accepting that if the earl's green-eyed monster inspired Trent to turn too quickly, she could be on the wrong end of the gambit. There was nothing to do but to make the most of the moment.

"No prospects or designs?" He shook his head. "I know my uncle presented me as a rustic but even if I had stumbled out of a bog, I couldn't believe that, Lady Wellcott."

"If there is more to the tale, I can assure you that this is not the time or place for it so you will have to take me at my word."

"I will take you at your word but I am inspired to engineer the time and place where I can hear all your tales, Lady Wellcott."

"Are you a clever enough engineer, Sir Tillman?" she asked. "Because when it comes to keeping secrets, like most women, I pride myself on the labyrinth I've constructed to hide them away."

The music faded and their steps slowed. The admiration in his gaze was palpable and Serena fought not to hold her breath. "I love a challenge, Lady Wellcott."

He bowed over her gloved hand and they retreated along with the other couples from the floor. Serena's stomach was a tight knot as Lord Trent intercepted them with a smile that didn't warm his eyes.

"How are your toes, Lady Wellcott?" he demanded. "It looked deadly tight on that floor."

"I survived to fight another day, Lord Trent." Serena said and then curtsied. "It was a pleasure meeting you, Sir Tillman, and I do hope I have the chance to see you again at another insipid social gathering very soon."

Adam smiled. "I will see to it."

She turned to Geoffrey who was quick to take her gloved hand and kiss her knuckles, the gesture more theatrical than was warranted but she dared not smile. "Lord Trent, I think tonight you made me wonder if I shall rely less on luck and more on fate for my future. Thank you for the dance."

She left without giving Trent a chance to compose his reply and headed into the crowded salon to weave through the safety of the wallflowers and chaperones before slipping out to ask for her carriage to be brought around.

Lady Serena Wellcott held her head high, confident that she'd left both men wanting more.

* * *

ADAM STRETCHED his legs out on the carriage ride back to his uncle's town house and tried to ignore the ache at the small of his back. The journey to London had wreaked havoc on his back and he'd have gladly forgone the evening for a long hot soak in a bathtub—except for Lady Serena Wellcott.

*My God, she was like no woman I have ever seen! Lady Wellcott was a peacock in a room full of dull hens and damned if I don't have a new purpose in this hellish venture.*

"What are you smiling about over there?" Uncle Geoffrey asked. "Out with it. Tell me."

It was an irritating command but Adam swallowed his resentment to attempt a civil answer. "I was just contemplating how surprising it was to enjoy myself at a dance."

"Balls are always lively and only a dullard would sit in a pout and be miserable in good company." Uncle Geoffrey leaned back against the seat across from him and adjusted the small curtain for a better view of the passing streets. "You will have the way of it before long."

"Perhaps." Adam ignored the implied insult. He'd lived in London when he was working on a project to reinforce Brunel's famous tunnel under the Thames but there was no point in arguing with a man who saw him only as a workman with dirt under his nails. His uncle lived to bait him and his mother had warned him of her younger brother's delight in conflict and torment. He sighed and took a slow deep breath to balance out his nerves. "I'll just watch and learn."

"Wise man." Trent shifted forward as if to study him. "What did you think of Lady Wellcott?"

"She was very lively." He kept his expression neutral, unwilling to share any sign of his interest. "The daughter of a friend of yours, did you say?"

"The *bastard* daughter of a friend of mine," his uncle corrected him with relish.

The word landed like stone at Adam's feet and he held as still as he could to await the rest of it. "I see."

Uncle Geoffrey sighed dramatically. "No one speaks of it openly but then they can only guess at the facts. I have noted her rise in fortunes with some interest though she's angered more than one of the Old Guard by doing so well without a nod to marriage. Not that they would have sacrificed one of their precious male pups to a woman with a questionable pedigree! It's the principle of course."

"But she is a titled woman and—"

"Her father bought a title for her through some obscure legal maneuver and with a sly nod from the crown. Even if the decree is as flimsy as a dandelion in late summer, the obscene fortune he reportedly settled on her has silenced most questions." Trent sat back against the carriage's upholstered wall, openly content to demonstrate his mastery on the subject of Lady Serena Wellcott. "Even so, she is ridiculously popular no doubt for her social skills and keen wit. It is said that she possesses a talent for investing or business or some such, for every report of her worth increases which naturally means it is all a bunch of exaggerated false gossip and she is likely as poor as a wren. Women do like to waste money on fripperies and nonsense and no unmarried woman without legitimate family or the support of a husband can be truly wealthy."

Adam hated the word 'bastard' and it made no difference to him if the woman he'd met had been a street urchin in some former life. It was Adam's turn to contemplate a study of the man across from him. Uncle Geoffrey was deliberately trying to put him off of her. The question was why.

"It is generous of you to befriend her then, despite the unfortunate circumstances of her parentage and her current poverty." Adam did his best not to allow the sarcasm he felt to bubble up and taint his speech.

"Yes! Well, you will find that I am a very generous man at the end of the day!"

Adam chose to nod rather than risk a reply.

His uncle noticed none of his discomfort. "Don't worry, dear nephew. I tell you these things to prove that I am no monster but an ally and mentor to you. Lady Wellcott is a very sweet creature flawed by circumstances beyond her control but you are the next Earl of Trent. There will be dozens of debutantes and eligible heiresses clawing over themselves to reach you and before the season is over, you will struggle to recall what Lady Serena Wellcott looks like."

"I wasn't worried."

"No. Good. Tomorrow, we'll set about making our first social calls together and I'll introduce you to my inner circles. I want to take you to the Club and ensure that before the week is out, your calendar is overflowing with invitations and calls. How does that sound?"

*It sounds like I'd rather put my head in a vise.*

"Delightful," Adam said softly.

He turned his face to look out the window, the light from the street lamps creating strange halos in the gloom. He hated his uncle's talent for back-handed compliments and twisted games. In any other social sphere, he doubted his uncle's rudeness would fly but his title gained him a strange immunity where he was described indulgently as eccentric or difficult.

*God, if being an earl condemns you to becoming an ass, I think I'll jump off one of my own bridges before I inherit.*

Adam sighed. His uncle was a strange tyrant and his mother had long avoided her brother's company. She had begged him to refuse his uncle's invitation for the season but Adam was tired of shying from the situation. Adam was the kind of man who preferred to face things head on. He was determined to survey the man for himself and be better armed for whatever the future may hold.

No matter how the lines of succession lay, Adam wasn't convinced that Uncle Geoffrey didn't have a plan of his own to defy them all.

*And I wonder if that plan doesn't have something to do with the very lovely Lady Serena Wellcott. He's spitting protests about her suitability, but I wouldn't put it past the old bear to think of putting up a fight. Marriage to a young woman may yet produce a male heir and give him the chance to crow.*

*Except I could care less about being an earl and lording it over Oakwell Manor.*

*So he's boxing shadows.*

*Although...*

The memory of Lady Wellcott in his arms during their waltz snagged at his calm and made him doubt himself. If Lady Wellcott were the object of his uncle's affections, then Adam wasn't so sure he could cross his arms and indifferently watch that courtship. He had spent the rest of the evening trying to catch a glimpse of her in the mob and wrestled with disappointment.

*Uncle Geoffrey may think to put me off with his black slice of gossip about the lady but I don't care if her parents were tinkers or even currently residents of Newgate.*

*And I don't care what game my uncle is playing.*

*He needs to learn how to lose.*

# CHAPTER 8

"How was it then?" Pepper asked as she began the work of the ball gown's buttons and hooks. "Did you dance at all?"

"She danced." Phillip answered for her, interrupting the pair as he boldly came into the room to lean against the post of her great bed. "And looked ridiculously beautiful in that gown while she was at it."

Pepper's eyes widened in shock but she withdrew after her mistress nodded, but not before she gave Phillip a warning look.

Serena stepped out of the ball gown and lay it across the back of her vanity chair. "Phillip Warrick. If I didn't know better, I would say that you had foolishly just confessed to being at the Drakes' party tonight. Hiding in the drapery, were you?"

"And if I were?"

Serena gripped the edge of the table and forced herself to stay still. "Then you need to go. You have a home of your own in London, sir, or even better, a country estate to the west. I know that we have reconciled but it is clear you need to retreat until this business is done. I love you, Phillip. But you do not have permission to burst into my rooms as if you own me, and you do not have the right to interfere with my life. You are not the master here. You are not the *master* of me."

The air in the room grew very still and Phillip froze in place, a man unsure if it was safe to breathe. "I should have knocked."

"You should have stayed away from Drakes after I expressly forbid you to be there."

Phillip slowly held up his hands in surrender. "I am not used to being forbidden. You are not the only one adjusting to this arrangement but I overstepped. I am human, Raven. Every instinct is to champion you, to protect you somehow and—I can hardly do that pacing in my library."

"I don't need a champion."

"We've already had this fight, haven't we?"

She nodded. "Yes and you lost."

He smiled. "As usual. But if it helps, he didn't see me. I didn't interfere. I was there merely to be on hand in case..." His words trailed off as his confidence faded. "You are not invincible, Raven."

"I never had the illusion I was." Raven took a moment, doing her best to keep her anger out of her voice. "You were lucky tonight. A room that crowded has a way of churning you from one place to the next, and if the tide had carried you into Trent's path, what would you have said? What lies would you have told him? And how would you have kept him from latching back on to that old hatred?"

"I don't know."

She sighed. "If he sets on you again, then I have no chance." Serena crossed her arms. "You promised to stay away."

"I promised not to interfere. I didn't interfere." Phillip raked one hand through his hair betraying his total capitulation. "But you're right. It was foolish and risky and—childish. The worst part of it was the bitter reward of watching you like that. So beautiful and alluring and so completely... For the record, if that man you were dancing with was the nephew, then I hate Adam Tillman."

"You do not. You dislike him because he is handsome and that is a terrible reason to stomp and pout about over there like a sullen toddler."

"I can hate him if I want to, woman." Phillip's pout gave way to his own wry humor. "Even if it is only because he's intolerably too smart looking, I'm sure I'll find additional reasons as this nightmare unfolds. I can guarantee you that in one conversation with that ape, I'll come up with a dozen things to loathe about his character."

"Phillip." She approached him, wary of igniting another conflict but determined. "I meant what I said. You will have to leave." Serena leaned in to reach up to cradle his face in her hands before she went on, "It was too much to ask to think that you could distract yourself in London for the duration."

He slowly shook his head in protest. "You do not have the power to exile me."

"No. Only the power to beg you to do the right thing and go willingly. Just for this Season, Phillip, until Trent is dealt with."

Phillip closed his eyes. "I should never have complained about using the servant's entrance."

She smiled. "No, especially since if I weaken and send you a letter begging you to return then that is the door you will use when you call on me." She threaded her fingers up into the nape of his neck, deliberately teasing his skin to send a shiver down his spine. "Unless your pride forbids it, my darling."

He opened his eyes, the heat there a blend of desire and anger. "I should thank you for believing I still have my pride left to me."

"I love you, Phillip Warrick."

"I have never wanted to strangle you more than at this moment, Raven."

She shook her head slowly. "Phillip. You don't mean it. You are angry and you have every right to be angry. But make no mistake. It is the anger of a child who dislikes the punishment they have openly earned. Rail all you want, Warrick, but don't throw away all that we've fought so hard to gain—not for the sake of pride. I am not ending our love affair. I'm saying it's clear that your need to champion me and hover has proven a greater obstacle than you can overcome."

"That's not a crime."

"No. Love is never a crime, Phillip. The crime is mine. I cannot do what I must if I am constantly fearful of your interference or worse—of defending my actions to you when it is all said and done."

"Do you intend to seduce—"

She cut him off quickly with a kiss, a warm sweet bribe to secure his complete attention. "I vowed to be faithful and to love you and you alone. I gave you my fidelity, my love, my loyalty and my soul, Phillip Warrick. I vowed to keep no secrets from you and to do whatever I can to be safe. Do not destroy the trust between us by disregarding the promises I have already made! Do you doubt me so easily? One dance? My god, Phillip, however will you weather the years ahead? The myriad of social traps and careful games I will play?"

Phillip was the one to initiate the next kiss, deepening the contact and prolonging the sensation that the world was beginning to fall away. "I will weather them by remembering that kiss and the look in your eyes right now."

"Will you? I pray that's so." Serena reached up to touch his cheek. "Love is just the first battle. It's a war ahead to preserve that happiness."

Phillip sighed. "A bitter truth. Though I am not—accepting total exile, Raven Wells. I will stay in my own sphere and out of sight."

She smiled. "Not total exile but until you prove yourself trustworthy, let's consider that a threat I shall hold in reserve."

"Is there an appeals process?"

"After everything that we have been through, you and I, and everything you now know of me, are you truly willing to risk it and find out?" Serena looked up into his face and waited. "Well?"

"I stand resolutely corrected, my lady's obedient servant."

Serena touched his face again with the cool blades of her fingers. "You are irresistible in that state, my love."

"Thank God."

His humor returned and she could feel relief coursing through his touch. "Did you have a miserable time hiding in the ferns, dearest?"

He nodded, then sighed. "It was purgatory and I am nearly cured of the impulse to follow you, although…"

"Although?" she asked.

"Tell me is there any chance Tillman has a speech impediment? The intellect of a draft horse? For God's sake, give me something to cling to, woman!"

She struggled not to laugh. "Give me a moment."

"Come on. Anything!"

"May I lie and say he had bad breath?" she offered and he immediately pulled her more tightly against his chest.

"I will accept that lie with desperate relief," he said and then lifted her chin for a kiss. "My vanity is in shreds, Raven. Banished and reduced to waiting for news that you wish me to secretly beg entry to your bed at your whim and will... Kiss me and soothe my pride."

"Is that all it will take?"

He shook his head very slowly. "Wounds these deep? I may need a great deal of attention."

Serena slowly smiled. "I'm not sure you should be rewarded so quickly. After all, you were very disobedient."

"Then punish me, my darling."

"Yes. First, a punishment that you will never forget—and then a reward to warm your blood in the lonely weeks ahead."

He said nothing, but his eyes gleamed with wicked anticipation.

She never looked away from him as she retrieved the long satin sash from her discarded ball gown. She tugged the sash loose slowly, drawing it out and up until it trailed from her fingertips all the way to the carpeted floor.

His breath caught and when Serena heard it, a rush of power surged through her body. *Here. Here was a new way to be conquered.* For by ruling him, she would surrender herself and she was smart enough to see it.

She stepped closer and reached up on her tiptoes to press the sash against his eyes. Phillip bent over to allow it, helping her to knot the swath of material behind his head to render him blind although not helpless. He was vulnerable however and the excitement of this shift affected them both.

She kissed him.

Then stepped back to finish undressing. Phillip reached for her. "Come here, woman!"

"No." She eluded him easily. "Behave."

He couldn't see but he could hear the soft weight of her corset falling to the floor and she deliberately stood close enough for him to feel the elusive brush of materials or shift in the air to hint at her movements.

Then it was her turn to undress him. She was an exotically distracting valet as she worked on each button, touching him far more than the task warranted and sending his pulse racing as he tried to anticipate the brush of her fingertips or the path of her attentions. At last, he was as naked as the day of his birth though there was nothing innocent in his stiffening cock or the taut lines of his body.

She took his hand and led him toward the bed, and he smiled. After all, here was more familiar territory and blindfolded or not, Phillip was comfortable in the knowledge that he could hold his own.

"Kneel."

Serena applied a small amount of pressure atop his shoulders to indicate that she wished him to lower to the floor. He obeyed but lost some of his confidence. They hadn't achieved the bed and he wasn't sure what adventure could follow if he was simply set on the floor.

She sat on the edge of the bed in front of him and within a single second, his imagination cleared the gate. Serena guided his hands to demonstrate that he was kneeling to face her, her thighs parted wide, her sex open to him, the scent of her arousal so close he instantly grasped his "task".

He could feel the tops of her stockings, the ribbons making an indent in the flesh of her thighs and trailing down to touch his bare shoulders and arms. The saucy choice to keep them on added color and depth to the increasingly naughty images his mind conjured of her beauty. He could "see" in perfect clarity the pink moist folds and the taut darker pink nub of her clit rising up in its tiny hood.

"Hands behind your back, please."

He needed no guidance to find her with his mouth.

He mapped out her sex in a glorious tactile game of feast and famine. He tasted and teased, happy to play along with his hands behind his back and to use only his mouth to please her. She was the perfect blend of salty sweetness and Phillip adored the flavor of her, marveling at how she subtly changed with her arousal until he could actually taste her excitement and the moment before her release.

His tongue lathed her clit in an insistent pattern, every stroke up, down and across, but never lingering too long on her pearl directly, until he feared he'd pushed her too fast. Her fingers spasmed and gripped his hair, and she began to keen and cry as her hips bucked and writhed against his mouth.

Serena moved forward against him to increase the pressure then shimmied away when the pleasure became so exquisite it bordered on pain.

Power.

Control.

She wanted it. She wanted all of it and then when she began to come, she wished for nothing more than to surrender the reins. The red hot coil inside of her began to release and she wanted him to be with her as it happened.

"Enough! Oh, you….are free! Come, ride me! Ride this fire with me!" Serena reached down to pull off his blindfold, eager to end the game but Phillip pulled the sash loose only to loop it over her wrists, shifting her back onto the bed beneath him and then drawing the long tie over the opposite bed post to trap her arms gently over her head.

She didn't care. If it meant that he would mount her, and fill the void inside of her, she'd have allowed him any liberty.

"Phillip!"

He moved back over her, parting her thighs and she lifted her bottom up to try to precipitate the rogering she desired, but he lowered himself over her, kissing the inside of thighs, the arch of her instep, then the side of her outer thighs, the indent of her hips, the rise of her belly. She'd have struck him in her frustration if the dratted man didn't know every secret place on her body that kept her temper in check.

Or rather somewhat in check.

"Hurry!"

"No."

She had commanded him too much. His obedience had been given but he would give no more. Tonight he would take his leave but not before he had made his mark on her soul, before he'd go. He untied her but only to shift her position.

"You wish a ride? Then let's have a ride, Raven."

He guided her to sit astride his hips, his cock an upright invitation for the lady to do as she pleased.

Serena did not need to be asked twice.

She knelt above him, savoring for just one moment the way the silken hot head of him notched against her flesh, before she lowered herself onto him, gasping at the intense mix of pleasure and pain as her body fought to stretch for him and to hold him. She shuddered as a sweet flood of heat uncoiled between her hips again and she was slick and soft with her own arousal.

He pressed his fingers into his hips as he lifted up, adding to the sensation of fullness and goading her to move. Serena smiled before she reached up to pull her hair back and up from her face, wishing him to see her wickedness as she shamelessly rode him.

His breath caught in his throat and she knew the gesture had achieved its aims. Of course, it also lifted her breasts and arched her back to make a pretty picture for the man. The advantages of vanity had finally come into play.

The ride became a full gallop quickly and Serena reached down to bring his hands up to breasts and then to bring his fingertips to her mouth where she could suckle them, mirroring the wet thrust and grip of her body with her lips. It was an unorthodox notion but she was immediately rewarded as he thickened inside of her, his excitement unmistakable.

If he'd meant to slow her, the notion was abandoned now.

He rolled her off and finally buried himself into her, each thrust another step toward an impossible climax. The grip of her muscles were so hot and so tight, Phillip gave in to raw desire and forgot to care for anything—for punishments or rewards, or for anything beyond the moment. He came so hard it robbed him of air and he would have sworn he saw sparks of light behind his eyes only to taste his own blood in his mouth, apparently from biting down on his tongue.

*Jesus. Why does that seem fair?*

She meant to banish him.

She meant to tell him good-bye.

All he could do was love her and make sure that whatever mark he could make in her world, it would be an indelible one.

AFTERWARD, they lay with their limbs entwined and Serena lazily trailed her fingers across his chest and arms, mapping his body in a sensual survey.

"What are you thinking?" he asked softly.

"I'm thinking that it is frightening how simple the scheme against Trent may be, but I have learned that complicated plans are always riskier and if there is a direct path open, it is never unwise not to consider it."

"But if it's too simple... Trent is as wily as a fox and may be leading you on a merry chase for his own amusement."

"Possibly." She conceded the point, then stretched out like a cat. "I'll have to play along to see."

"No more secrets. Tell me what you have in mind."

She leaned up to sit next to him in a nest of the bedding, her knees drawn up like a child's. "Unless my instincts are wrong, Trent is eyeing me as if he believes he has a chance at bedding me—or even wedding me, if that is his aim."

Phillip closed his eyes with a groan. "God, I may be sick."

"If I allow him to believe that I am still loyal to him, if I vaguely allude to some lingering affection without overplaying it, then I'll have the whip hand. And if I then turn my attentions to his nephew, I am fairly sure that the play will write itself."

Phillip sat up, leveraging his body to sit across from her. "Ignoring how much I already don't like you flirting with Tillman, I think you're

RENEE BERNARD

underestimating how savagely Trent will turn, teeth bared, if he thinks you've betrayed him."

"Of course he will. How could he not? It will all echo his past too closely as he is once again bested by a younger man but this time from within his family. It already chafes him to grow older and to see Adam stepping into his place. But when Adam looks to be mocking his virility and taking the woman he wants, this time, I will make sure I twist that point cruelly home until all Trent can see is red." Serena sighed in pleasure as the chilling plan came together. "It was you he went after, remember? Not his mistress. Not the woman who flirted with another man and invited you into her bed. He blamed *you*."

"Yes. So?"

"In his mind, women are pawns not players. So, it will be Tillman that he blames. If I drive him mad with rage and provoke him so that there is no biding his time in some grand scheme, then I can push him into fast and unthinkable action. Like a sick animal, he will feed on his own flesh and blood and be forced to face the consequences of the feast."

"No. It's too much."

She shook her head. "It will be whatever Trent chooses. But if I'm right, at the very least, he will be socially destroyed for his actions against his heir."

"What more would you expect?"

"If there is violence and he ends his own bloodline, then I might expect a front row seat at his hanging, Phillip. Not that I would wish for it, but Trent is dangerous and unpredictable and I would be foolish not to steel myself against the very worst that fate might serve up."

Phillip's breath caught in his throat. Raven looked like a pagan goddess in the moonlight, sitting amidst her bedding with her black hair tumbling wild down her bare shoulders and back. But this goddess was casting a spell as she spoke of mayhem and blood and he felt helpless to stop any of it. A hidden part of him admired the ruthless cast of her mind but a shiver of ice worked down his spine.

"I asked, didn't I?"

"You don't approve?" she asked.

"No, I don't approve. But I said no more secrets. I just—you aren't a murderer, Raven."

"No. Not yet." Her expression was impossible to read. "The plan is still evolving. You asked what I was thinking and I told you. That's all."

"Yes, but you're thinking of setting Trent up to murder his own nephew!"

"I don't expect it to come to the worst. Sir Tillman is not a sausage-fingered child to be overtaken in a fight. If! If it came to such a moment, he'll defend himself and the only one who will be hurt will be the earl."

Phillip shook his head. "You don't know that for certain. It's all a guess, isn't it?"

She shuddered, turning her face away from him. "I don't want to talk about it anymore."

"I may dislike Adam for the way he looked at you at Drake's and how lovely you looked in his arms but...I don't wish him any harm."

"I don't wish him any harm either," she whispered. "Just leave it."

"The earl isn't the only one who could be hurt. Can't you see how this tears at your own soul? You aren't just moving chess pieces around a board. You toy with putting an innocent man in the path of a madman and—"

"I don't want to fight about this, Phillip!"

"No?"

"No. A fight insinuates that I have an opinion or position that is under threat of being overturned and that I have to defend myself, or that I need to change your mind. You can say whatever you want, Warrick, but I am already on this journey and my path is set in stone. I will have my revenge against Trent."

Phillip climbed off the bed, his movements jerking and betraying his fury as he retrieved his clothes and dressed. "Your path. Your terms. Your revenge. God, how the hell does a man come to this? I should just shoot Trent on the street and spare us all!"

"Phillip! You'll do no such thing! Getting yourself hanged, are you mad?" She scrambled to follow him, shedding useless modesty to reach him, naked and vulnerable. "Please, Phillip. You swore to love me, to give me this, to let me do what I needed to do! I need *all* of it. Not one part or piece, but all of it to move forward in this world and to survive. You left me. I left you. Hear me when I say that I don't want to know what is on the other side of truly losing you."

"Raven."

"Once I was Spring itself, wasn't I? Help me, Phillip. Help me not to become Winter."

He pulled her into his arms, one last time, once more before his exile, both of them desperate to push away the inevitable.

ALONE IN THE grey of predawn, Serena stared up at the ceiling. Phillip's departure had come at last and she marveled that this time, the impact was less. No doubt because he had left with tender words, with both of them whispering eternal pledges of their love and vowing to reunite as soon as possible. And no doubt because she was the founder of it all, and the one holding the power to end their separation with a single summons.

She wasn't as cold or calculating as she'd deliberately seemed to him. Speculating aloud about the worst possible scenarios served more than one purpose. She knew from past experience that not being prepared for the bleakest outcomes left her too vulnerable and allowed for too many mistakes. It was better to include the nightmares early so that they could be potentially avoided.

But there was no getting around it.

Phillip Warrick was going to be tested to his limits and softening the blows with deception wouldn't serve either of them. If their love was going to survive, then it would have to withstand the deadly fire ahead.

*I am no murderer.*

*Oh, God. Not yet.*

# CHAPTER 9

$S$erena dressed for her day's outing with Pepper's assistance, a new clarity and calm enveloping her senses. With Phillip's cooperative retreat, she was a woman freed of constraint.

But not of conscience.

"Sleep well then?" Pepper asked brightly.

"I must have," Serena replied, eyeing the deceptive glow in her own cheeks. By all rights she should have laid abed until the luncheon bell rang, but she felt like a colt straining against the traces. "I am eager to see where the day leads."

"Shall I have Donovan ready the carriage for the park?"

"Yes but not for the park. I will have the top down to enjoy the weather, but there is an exhibit at the museum I am planning to take in. I wish to make an innocent turn out with Harriet. After all, Lady Serena Wellcott cannot always be seen dancing, Pepper."

Pepper shook her head as she finished the row of covered buttons at the back of Serena's back. "No man worth kissing is going to waste a pretty day like today standing about some musty paintings and lifeless stone heathens prancing about in their birthday suits!"

"Pepper!" Serena gave her friend a look of mock horror. "Why would I spoil a day at the museum with male company? And where in the world did you get the idea that any man is truly 'worthy' of kissing?"

"Aren't they?" Pepper asked breathlessly.

"No." Serena struggled to keep her expression serious. "And even if a man did earn a kiss or two, it would be a foolish woman who would allow him to think they were his due. Men are already too full of their own power, Prudence, and a man worthy of kissing is usually the one who thinks to deserve it least."

Pepper crossed her arms, a mischievously defiant student. "That's a mash of nonsense! I am not bestowing kisses on any hangdog of a man who doesn't see his own way to it!"

Serena smiled, openly pleased at the flash of spirit in her maid's eyes. Whatever ghosts remained from her experience at Southgate appeared to be banished, once and for all. "I stand corrected."

"Yes, well," Pepper's hands fell to her hips. "I know better but at least you stand ready for the day."

Serena made a quick turn to check Madame Montellier's latest creation. Periwinkle blue silk, so rich it looked like liquid, shimmered and gleamed, artful cascades of pleats and Pauline's delicate florets completed the spring-like effect of the bustle. She sighed. "It seems cruel to wear anything this pretty knowing that Harriet will be dressed like a crow."

"Lady Lylesforth prefers it that way. She likes the way you divert attention away from her and she'd thank you for it if she wasn't too starched to say it."

Serena swallowed a gasp at Prudence's insight. *Wisdom from my dear girl and a good lesson that nothing is missed in the world below of the world above.* "Then the opal hair comb and pins, Pepper, and the matching bonnet."

Pepper added the hair ornaments and hat to her mistress's black curls, the arrangement completing the image of a well-bred, refined English noblewoman. "There. Watch that those stone statues don't come to life to bother you, for I swear you are that lovely!"

Serena blushed. "It's an innocent turn but thank you, Pepper. Now, enjoy your afternoon off."

Pepper gifted her with a saucy curtsey. "I will and without a moment wasted."

WHEN SHE ARRIVED at Lady Lylesforth's to collect her friend, Serena was met with the unfortunate news that Harriett had come down with a terrible cold overnight and would not be able to accompany her. Serena sought assurance that a physician was in attendance and that there was nothing else she could do before deciding to face the day alone.

"Is she not coming?" Her footman, Albert, asked.

"No, so if you will plan on alighting with me at the museum, I would be grateful."

"Yes, Your Ladyship, with pleasure."

At the museum, she purchased the tickets and then savored the rare treat of a solitary stroll amidst the glorious splendor of Europe's masters. Albert, or Bertie, trailed respectfully after her, an attendant only should she require one. Serena glanced back and smiled at the realization that the man was agog in awe, gaping at the paintings in wonder and a bit lost to the room's treasures.

*I should bring Pepper. Fuss or no, she could stand with a bit of exposure to the finer things and it would do her some good to—*

"Lady Wellcott?"

Serena turned, instantly recognizing the voice and awash in adrenalin at the surprise. "Sir Tillman, what an unexpected delight!" It wasn't entirely a lie. It wasn't unpleasant to see him but she truly hadn't anticipated his presence and the tactical part of her mind reeled. There had been no word from her informants on Portman Square that the earl or his nephew would emerge before tomorrow night's card game at Pellbrooks and not to see an exhibit on European masters' oil paintings.

"You do not have your elderly chaperone with you today?"

"My elderly chaperone?" Serena blinked in surprise.

"I haven't met her but from Uncle Geoffrey's description, she is quite fierce." Adam replied. "I was already impressed with anyone who can make a grown man sulk and wished to thank her for it."

Serena smiled as Harriet had apparently rankled the earl into describing her like a crusted old biddy. She would omit arguments for Lady Lylesforth's beauty only for the simple mischief it would provide when Adam did finally meet her. "She is home with a cold today but I will convey your gratitude, Sir Tillman. And you? Is Lord Trent not with you then?"

Adam's smile mirrored hers. "Uncle Geoffrey would rather submit to a beating than ten minutes in an art museum."

Relief flooded through her frame and her heart rate slowed accordingly. She was skilled at thinking on her feet but loathed surprises. "Surely he is not so bad as that, though I do recall him saying once that he was not fond of activities that dictated everyone would be looking at the walls and not at the splendor of his waistcoat."

"You know him remarkably well, Lady Wellcott."

Serena smiled. "No. I know him only as well as most and no better which hints that I know almost nothing of him. Your uncle is not as open as he seems."

They fell into step and strolled toward the next painting before stopping.

"Do you mind if I ask you a question, Lady Wellcott?"

"No. You may ask me anything you wish."

"What do you think of my uncle? I mean…are you fond of his person, Lady Wellcott?"

She looked up at him. "Fond? I confess that particular question has me at a loss. Why do you ask such a thing?"

Raven held her breath. Elaborate schemes were the work of fools. Suddenly she knew that simplicity would be her master and there would be no margin for error. She decided to be as honest as she could with Adam. She would make it clear that she was not in pursuit of him for a match, guaranteeing that his feelings were well clear of the looming battlefield.

Even when his uncle was injured by his misperceptions and madness, Adam would remain intellectually free of the entanglements and would be better armed against his uncle's unsubstantiated accusations.

She knew what it felt like to be used in a scheme for revenge and had no desire to inflict it on another human being. She would guard Adam's peace of mind if she could and see if Trent's destruction couldn't occur like an unforeseen bolt of lightning.

Because she liked him too much already.

The challenge would be to not like him more.

"My uncle is..." Adam sighed. "He is a great admirer of yours."

She smiled but shook her head. "Perhaps in the way a person admires a Persian cat."

"I think there is more to it than that," Adam said. "When he speaks of you..."

"What has he told you of me?" she asked him directly.

"Nothing of importance."

There was something in his tone that snagged at her attention and her steps slowed to a halt, forcing him to do the same and to face her. "Sir Tillman. I wish to know what he said, whether it is of consequence or not and the reason I have asked such a thing is that I am hopeful of your friendship and I demand honesty from my friends, sir."

"I think he meant to put me off which makes me wonder if he sees me as a rival for your affections."

"He sees every man breathing as a rival in this world, Sir Tillman. But how did he try to put you off?" Serena asked.

"He indicated that you are—that the circumstances of your birth were not ideal." Adam shifted his weight from one foot to the other, openly uncomfortable. "As I said, it is nothing of importance—not in my estimation, Lady Wellcott."

She smiled. "Then you are a unique soul in this cynical world, Sir Tillman."

"Uncle Geoffrey has demonstrated a certain resemblance to an old crone when it comes to any opportunity for gossip." Adam swallowed in distaste. "That is if his speeches make any sense at all."

"Sir Tillman, for all his faults, I should be grateful to him for revealing what I would have considered an embarrassing admission. I was not the product of a sanctified marriage but I am not ashamed of my father, for he has been very generous to me. As my former guardian, Lord Trent, rarely hesitates to hint at his opinions regarding my limitations. I suspect he told you less to make a claim and more to guarantee that you saw my faults as well and didn't waste your time on an undesirable creature."

"What?" It was Adam's turn to stop in his tracks. "What did you just say about guardians?"

"The Earl of Trent." Serena tipped her head back to reply. "I was in your uncle's care as a child for a few years until I came of age." She took a small step back. "I…am so sorry, Sir Tillman. Was I too familiar and too quick to speak?"

"No. There is nothing to apologize for. I just can't believe he never mentioned—not to anyone that he even…had a ward." Adam shook his head in disbelief.

"He *never* informed his family of my existence?" Serena echoed his disbelief with a touch of her own. "All this time I assumed that he would have made a private show of his generosity but it makes more sense…"

"Does it?"

Serena swallowed. Of course it made sense to say nothing to his relatives if he'd truly meant to use her in a scheme and dispose of her in a marriage poisoned with his lies. If Warrick had strangled her on their wedding night, Trent would have danced a jig and publicly made a theatrical show of his shock and horror at the loss of his penniless orphaned ward. Years of isolation and having never met the earl's family, yet she'd never really surmised how marginally she'd been placed on the board.

"Yes," Serena replied and then attempted a smile. "It was a temporary arrangement, after all. I was a knobby kneed child and what difference in the greater scheme of things to a man like your uncle?

Perhaps it is a sign of his better qualities to be so discreet and not to seek praise for his gesture."

"I've always imagined him rattling around Oakwell on his own, like a strange ghost." Adam ran a hand through his hair, unsettling his curls. "God, what a twist!"

She shook her head. "A small twist."

"I don't understand. He spoke of you after the Drakes as if he had experienced a reunion but how is that possible? Would he not have kept in touch with you?"

"No. Lord Trent does not subscribe to sentimental rituals. Once I was of age and my father offered to intervene in my care, it was made clear that I should not trouble the earl further. I have not seen or spoken to him in several years, and in light of his aversion to feminine correspondence, I have respectfully failed to send a single letter."

"My God!"

Serena blinked as if confused. "Lord Trent never complained of my absence or silence, Sir Tillman. I hope do not judge me harshly for relinquishing etiquette without protest."

"It's not you I judge. But how can a man be such a great part of a young girl's life, nearly a parent, and then…be nothing?"

"I was a charitable case. That is all." She spoke openly, softening pain with a feminine smile. "The education he provided and experiences of Oakwell Manor made me the woman I am today, Sir Tillman. I am naturally grateful to Lord Trent for his generosity and he knows it. I told him as much at Drake's."

"I'll never comprehend him."

"Don't try." Serena glanced at a display of Egyptian funeral urns. "If I know anything of the earl, I know that he loathes looking back, even at people who may be part of that landscape. It would be useless vanity on my part to demand more of him or complain if I failed to stand out from his rose bushes."

Adam watched her, marveling at how calm and self-possessed she appeared. There was more to the story, but he had no desire to injure her with a hundred questions that would only confirm Uncle Geoffrey's eccentric disregard. Her confession explained the strange possessive tone his uncle used when speaking of Lady Wellcott.

"I've grown up with the man as a distant figure with as much familial affection as I might have for a stranger." He pretended to read a placard about hieroglyphs and then cleared his throat. "Was my existence also kept a secret from you?"

Silence answered him and Adam looked up to see her distress as she struggled to come up with phrasing that would spare him. The very notion that she would worry more about his own feelings than her own froze him in place.

She shook her head. "Persian cats are lovely company but I'm sure the earl thought private information about his family wasn't appropriate to—"

"Don't do that. Don't defend him."

"Never." She straightened her shoulders. "It is a fault of mine to speak as I find. So I will say, Sir Tillman, I'm glad we can be so honest with each other. You know the worst of me and what I alluded to at the ball. Perhaps you also feel some relief at all these revelations?"

"Relief?"

"That I told you the truth. That I am not another scheming woman in your path after your title or your inheritance. It is obvious why I am the last woman who would raise her hand to try to catch your attention or insinuate myself into your sphere but I am pleased to think that we can be friends all the same."

"Nothing is obvious beyond my confusion that there isn't a trail of men following your every move, Lady Wellcott."

"I've dismissed them, Sir Tillman. The fortune hunters who are interested in my money enough to ignore my history will never win my heart. And for the sons of my father's peers, I am disqualified by birth, no matter what my dear father has arranged."

"It's a black mark you've overcome and if your popularity is any indication, then there's no impediment to any match you desired."

She sighed. "I am accepted socially and have gained my standing *because* I have made it clear that I don't desire a match. I am no threat to any matron, debutante or dowager and have managed my welcomes very carefully. If they saw me as a predatory interloper, it would all change."

"So you move among them and they allow it because you aren't playing the game?" he asked softly.

Something in her chest tightened but she kept her expression neutral. "Even so. That was quite a speech I made, wasn't it?"

He nodded. "I'm going to take a while to digest several of those points before I fully respond, Lady Wellcott."

"As you wish," she conceded. "But for now, I want you to tell me how you would design a museum, if you had the commission or what innovations you would suggest for a modern home."

*HOLY HELL.*

They'd politely parted ways after finishing their stroll through the galleries, and he'd ignored civility and stared after her like a man watching the sails of a ship after being marooned.

*How is such a woman possible?*

She'd quoted philosophers and poets, known more about the paintings and artwork than the curator, yet never seemed over-bearing in her opinions. She'd drawn him into an extensive conver-sation on the design of public spaces until he'd finally caught himself in the midst of an impassioned speech about light vectors and realized that he'd surrendered reason completely. Her footman was yawning ten paces behind her and Lady Serena Wellcott was nodding as enraptured as if he were spinning words into butterflies.

He prided himself on being a practical man, grounded in the sciences and engineering but one afternoon with Lady Wellcott and he was a bemused fool.

She'd been Uncle Geoffrey's ward.

A fact that Uncle Geoffrey hadn't thought worth mentioning even as he'd vomited the truth about her illegitimate birth and made it clear that she was 'off the table'.

But nothing about Serena seemed unworthy and his uncle's opinions were easily ignored. *Hell, Uncle Geoffrey's opinions weigh as much as a sneeze in my reckoning!*

But she'd proudly reinforced things by stating her ineligibility and disinterest in a match of any kind. She was a woman who offered him a friendship without strings and without a single promise or hint of more.

Things should have been as clear as a pane of glass.

But nothing was clear.

He wanted to confront his uncle for an accounting of himself but something in him shied away from the notion. *To what end? To confirm that the man is a heartless bastard? Or that he truly played the role of benevolent benefactor to a woman I wish him to have no part of—that I don't want to share even in retrospect?*

*If there's a consolation it's that she and I have more in common with our odd ties to Uncle Geoffrey and our common disregard for him than any differences.*

Adam shifted to walk back into the gallery, unwilling to return home.

*A woman like that would never give Uncle Geoffrey her hand.*

*Unless...*

Unless his uncle thought to twist whatever gratitude he sensed a woman in her position should have into a misguided sense of loyalty or honor. Lady Serena Wellcott appeared long past such a gambit and far too independent to fall prey to that ploy but Adam struggled with a growing sense of unease.

For there was something else at play and another element flowing underneath it all.

His brow furrowed at the tangled storms of supposition that gathered inside him. A replica of the "Rape of the Sabine Women" didn't add any calm to his spirit as he was confronted with a woman's desperation frozen for all time in marble. The maiden's hands were outstretched upward to an uncaring heaven against the horror of brutal male hands and Adam shuddered.

The sight made him thankful to Providence that he wasn't as vulnerable as a woman to the uncaring villainy of others. He tried to imagine what Serena's life would have held if his uncle hadn't taken her into his protection. Even an indifferent guardian was better than the unshielded life of a woman alone in this world.

It was too early to tell what his uncle's intentions were toward Serena.

But he suspected he knew his own.

*If Uncle Geoffrey tries to hurt her, then he will answer to me.*

# CHAPTER 10

"*D*euce!" Serena laid her cards out and clapped her hands. Her luck had held firm at the tables at Pellbrooks' card party and she was secretly pleased. She'd meant to honestly and fairly lose a small fortune if the night required it, but instead some mischievous god of luck had alighted on her shoulder and she was basking in the sensation. She was also enjoying the cocoon of feminine respectability at her table. Harriet was still too unwell to accompany her and so Serena had improvised to ensure that there was no opportunity for aspersions to be cast on her character. Ursula was tentative in her wagers but Lady Hodge-Clarence added her gravitas to every hand if not any witty conversation.

Ursula's sister-in-law, a Mrs. Foxwood, tossed her cards down with an ungracious sigh. "If it were a game of skill, I should have a chance of winning! But this is a devil's snare!"

"Temperance!" Ursula chided her archly. "Not fifteen minutes ago you were boring me to tears with your excitement over this activity. I find it interesting that your enthusiasm wanes with your purse."

Temperance pressed her lips together so tightly they disappeared. "An unkind observation is hardly a comfort."

Serena smiled. "Perhaps the comfort is that luck is a fickle friend

91

and may just as quickly delight you, Mrs. Foxwood, if you stay the course?" Serena leaned over slightly, "My beginner's luck is the first to fade."

Temperance was unconvinced. She folded her arms, a humorless pout overtaking her already unattractive features. "Easy to smile when one is apparently the easy victor, but I am inclined to think there are better ways to spend an evening than this sinful pursuit."

Serena put her cards down gently. "What hobbies and entertainments do you prefer, Mrs. Foxwood?"

"God, if you think I'm going to abandon cards for embroidery," Ursula said crisply, "you have lost the last of your grip on reality, woman."

Temperance's pout solidified into a genuine snit complete with tear-filled eyes and Serena finally decided that it was time to intervene. "The smoke has begun to irritate my throat, ladies. Would you like to accompany me, Temperance? On a walk about the house toward the terraces?"

Temperance managed a curt nod and stood from the table, then in a rush to escape Ursula's censure, sailed off without waiting for Serena. Serena smiled at the awkward shock on Lady Hodge-Clarence's face and made her own hurried pursuit of her unlikely new companion.

"Mrs. Foxwood," Serena hailed her softly. "If you don't slow down, the other guests will think we are playing chase."

Temperance obeyed but not cheerfully. "I hate card parties."

"So I guessed."

Serena followed Temperance as she withdrew to the other side of the salon away from the crowded tables.

Mrs. Foxwood turned without warning to stop for conversation and Serena had to avert herself from stumbling into the woman. "Lady Wellcott. Who are you precisely?"

"Pardon?" The question was so abrupt, Serena gasped at it.

"One hears...such vague tales in London. You appear out of nowhere a few years ago with a pedigree and no history. Your fortunes must be exaggerated as you appear to have no family and certainly, no husband. I should think you a courtesan to kings the way you present yourself with your elegant attire and striking sense of fashion but—Ursula refers to you like some kind of inviolate pillar of moral standing and several friends and acquaintances seem to be under the impression that you are an angel above reproach. They speak of you in raptured tones that make me wonder how a woman earns that kind of regard." Temperance's scrutiny was emotionless and unfaltering. "You are a mystery, Lady Wellcott."

"Am I?" Serena blinked. "My goodness, I had no idea!"

"Did you not?" Temperance said evenly. "Yet, I still long to hear your answer."

"My answer to…" Serena took a slow soft breath to regain her mental footing. Temperance wasn't the first but it had been a while since she'd been so openly challenged. "I apologize, Mrs. Foxwood, but did you mean to ask me if I were a saint or a—" Serena swallowed as if the giving voice to the very word were abhorrent to her, "*Courtesan?*"

"Are you?"

"I am neither!" Serena stiffened her spine, giving righteous indignation full rein, deliberately not lowering her voice. "But I am most assuredly not a whore! And I will sue anyone for slander who would have it otherwise! How dare you repeat such a thing!"

"What is this?" Lady Pellbrooks stood from her game to cross the room. "Ladies, what discord has poisoned your evening?"

Temperance's stance changed instantly, as the withering gaze of her sister-in-law and her hostess combined to make her rethink her candor. "I meant…only to learn more of…Lady Wellcott."

"Mrs. Foxwood thinks me too well dressed or elegantly appointed to be a well-bred lady of quality," Serena said more quietly, allowing an open show of her injured spirit to sell her vantage point and turning to her hostess to kiss her cheek and begin her retreat. "Thank you for including me in this lovely evening, Lady Pellbrooks, but I have no desire to disrupt the proceedings by sparking unwarranted curiosity and speculation by simply wearing the wrong jewels."

Mrs. Foxwood's pout returned. "Foolish theatrics over nothing, if you ask me."

"No one asked you, Mrs. Foxwood!" Lady Hodge-Clarence was not pleased as she sailed up. "Temperance, tell me you have not insulted the esteemed Lady Wellcott!"

"I have not." Mrs. Foxwood could only cling to what ground she had left. "I merely asked about her family connections and social standing and it was interpreted as a call to war."

"What's this?" A male voice entered the fray and the women shifted in surprise.

Serena's expression was calm but there was nothing welcome in the Earl of Trent's arrival at the party in this moment in time. Chaos was a drug to him, and she could only pray that he wouldn't take grim striking pleasure in adding to it with a dash of his own.

"Lady Wellcott! Have I arrived late only to miss a good brawl?" Geoffrey teased.

"No," Serena said as she tried to smile. "You are too clever to miss anything, your lordship. Please, enjoy the tables and do your best to show a touch of mercy to those poor gentlemen who haven't yet experienced your gaming skills, but I will take my leave."

Geoffrey's brow furrowed. "You must stay, Lady Wellcott."

"Yes…" Lady Pellbrooks was making every effort to save the merry atmosphere of the night. "I'm sure Mrs. Foxwood was about to apologize for her…"

Ursula cleared her throat. "For her early departure and wretched luck. Come, Temperance. I have a headache and you will graciously accompany me." Lady Hodge-Clarence gripped her sister-in-law's elbow. "We look forward to seeing you at the concert next week, Lady Pellbrooks. Don't we, Mrs. Foxwood?"

Temperance nodded, a woman temporarily cowed into obedience. "Yes. We count the hours."

The two women left and Serena's watched in sympathy, aware that if Mrs. Foxwood weren't regretting her words that she would before she escaped Lady Hodge-Clarence's carriage.

*For which I am sorry, Temperance, but this may be the least of your troubles.*

"I should return to my game." Lady Pellbrooks stepped back. "Let me direct you to my husband's table, Lord Trent. He will be so pleased to see you, and the Marquis of—"

"Do not trouble yourself, Lady Pellbrooks." The earl smiled, waving her offer away. "I am never shy and will make my own way, have no fear. But with your permission, I will petition Lady Wellcott to linger for a while."

Lady Pellbrooks left them with a smile, her party's atmosphere restored.

She allowed the earl to pull her aside but only so far as private conversation required. Serena was without Harriet and was not about to risk the loss of an audience if she needed one. "I will not stay long."

"Come on, duchess, you can't let a pinched little ferret like Foxwood send you running!" Geoffrey chided. "She's nothing."

Serena shook her head. "She is not nothing. She is a woman with a good reputation, related solidly either by marriage or by blood to no less than three Peers of the Realm and if my memory serves, I think she is on the musical advisory committee for Westminster's boys choir or some such. I am surprised at you, your lordship, for dismissing such a dangerous creature." She smiled mischievously. "You are a brave soul."

"Ha! I am your knight in shining armor!"

"Truly." Serena sighed. "But for me, retreat is the better part of valor in this instance."

"Nonsense. You were victorious," Geoffrey protested. "Come play cards."

"I am not the victor." Serena looked at him, swallowing the bile that rose in her throat. Here was the man that invoked her bastardy when it suited him, or called her duchess when it pleased him, but she was the one who walked the narrow ledge between nobility and scandal. "A married woman of any station will always take precedence over me and I will always suffer their scrutiny." She sighed again, forcing a merrier smile onto her face. "It is your fault for spoiling me, Lord Trent. I think too much of myself to suffer fools lightly."

"That is as it should be," he said. His eyes grew alight with pride. "You are exactly as I would have you."

Serena looked away, determined to deflect the direction of his thoughts or diffuse any flirtation. "And where is Sir Tillman? Are you going to teach him how to empty your friends' pockets?"

"He is—"

"Here," Adam supplied as he approached. "Wishing it were billiards but I am prepared to hold my own."

The earl's mood instantly changed. "Billiards! Billiards excludes the participation of the ladies and is hardly a game for good company." He crossed his arms defensively. "What a notion!"

The muscle in Adam's jaw ticked but he said nothing.

"It is a gentleman's game, Lord Trent. Come, sir, be kind." She smiled at Adam, genuinely pleased to see him again. "I can see the appeal of billiards to an engineering mind."

"I enjoy a weekly night of it at the club despite my uncle's protests." Adam nodded. "But I should have been more sensitive, uncle. At your age, the strain of it is likely too much for your back."

Geoffrey's mouth fell open in protest but Serena spoke before poor Lady Pellbrooks was alerted to yet another battle in her grand drawing room. "Oh, no, you don't! Sir Tillman, your uncle is too wise to rise to that bait but no more quarrels. I have already caused too much of a stir this evening and have no wish to be banished from any future gatherings."

"Your presence will be missed." Adam looked down into her eyes and it was easy to smile back.

"I should wish you both luck tonight before I go then. A lady should know to take her leave when she is not at her best, and when her chaperones have deserted her. Good night, friends."

She departed before another round of explanations or apologies would be required and left Pellbrooks with her head held high.

"DAMN. There goes my only chance at decent conversation," Adam sighed.

Lord Trent shook his head. "I will do my utmost to not take that insult personally, boy. Though I agree, she should have stayed to improve my evening—not yours. I love it better when she spits in their eyes than when she plays the delicate lady."

Adam's attention immediately shifted back to his uncle. "You love nothing. Let's play cards."

"God! When did you become such a ball of black tar?" Lord Trent began to lead them into the room. "I should tell you that before you came in the lady accidentally admitted something I have long suspected."

"And what was that?" Adam asked.

"That she secretly longs to be married!" Trent whispered confidentially. "But then what woman doesn't? It is just as I said. Smoke and mirrors and all pretense when behind it all, every woman no matter how proud they appear longs to be tucked safely into a man's protection."

Adam's disbelief was so stark he could taste it. "Who would have guessed at such a thing?"

"*And* I'll have you know that I love...a great many things, you dullard!"

Adam held his tongue.

*You do love a great many things, Uncle.*

*But people are not things, are they?*

He glanced back at the room's entrance where she had gone, a growing sense of some missed opportunity, some lost moment in time. Uncle Geoffrey's nonsensical claim about Serena confessing some secret wish to wed was pure delusion but it unsettled his nerves.

*He is perhaps hearing what he wants to hear.*

*And that is never a good sign.*

97

# CHAPTER 11

Serena dropped her reticule on the table by her bed, the weight of her winnings making a small authoritative sound that made Pepper smile.

"I can't think of a person who has your luck…" Pepper sighed as she pulled out Serena's wraps and nightgown. "Though by that look on your face, I'd warrant not all the cards came up the way you were hoping tonight. Did the earl not attend?"

"He did. I saw him for just a moment as I was leaving." Serena turned her back to allow Pepper to help her undress. "I wasn't in the mood to play."

Pepper's eyes widened in surprise. Something off in her mistress's tone. "And Sir Tillman? Was he not in the mood for a hand or two?"

Serena's stillness spoke volumes. "I didn't inquire but I'm sure he can hold his own at a card party or make his own excuses if he wishes. He mentioned a penchant for billiards at his club and I don't blame him. Men are luckier in their vast choices to occupy their hours."

"A shame you couldn't—"

"Leave it." Serena cut her off, stepping away. "I'll finish this. I'm tired and out of sorts but I prefer to see myself to bed. Get some sleep, Pepper."

"As you wish." They had been together too long for Pepper to mistake the signs. Serena rarely admitted to anything remotely resembling fatigue or weakness. The demand for solitude was valid and she respected the request with smooth speed and without complaint.

She headed downstairs to ensure that all was well. The kitchen had long since quieted for the day and the house was almost silent. She left a note for the cook to anticipate Lady Wellcott's wishes for her breakfast tray and then glanced at the clock to note the time.

*Nearly midnight.*

Pepper headed down the empty servant's corridors to the house's back entrance where deliveries were made. She unlocked the portal and smiled. "You're on time."

"Why is she home early? I thought it was cards tonight?"

Pepper shook her head. "Hush! It was cards and she isn't sharing her every thought, is she? Not even with me, I'll have it known!"

He leaned against the doorframe, lowering his voice. "I apologize."

"God, she'd skin me alive if she knew I was doing this." Pepper smoothed her hands over her apron nervously.

"Prudence. It's my neck that stretches if she realizes this secret but you have my eternal gratitude for the risk you take, dear girl."

Pepper sighed. "Very well. There's not much to say but if I know her, the meat of the battle's just ahead. Trent's like a poison and even my lady isn't immune to it. Every minute with him is taking its toll and she won't suffer it much longer."

"She'll begin to push for a quick finish." He took off his top hat and raked his fingers through his hair, betraying his nerves. "Damn it. I can't help but fear that in a rush, mistakes are made and the danger of a misstep grows. And the nephew? Any signs he is even remotely a dullard?"

"Sir Warrick!" Pepper playfully swatted at his arm to cheer him. "Jealousy makes you far too pretty!"

He laughed softly. "Thank you. Now tell me something useful, Prudence."

"Sir Tillman prefers billiards to cards. I think he plays at his club. She's set for the Royal Theatre on Thursday, her dragon in tow if Lady Lylesforth is recovered from her cold. And...she is missing you dreadfully."

"You have no proof of that last one."

"I do! I'd wager my favorite bonnet on it!"

"You're that certain, are you?" he asked, his good humor returning. "Your favorite?"

"You'll buy me two if she doesn't admit it and send for you herself before the month is out! How is that for confident, sir?" Pepper put her hands on her hips, a woman unafraid.

"I'll buy you a dozen bonnets."

Pepper's merriment faltered. "Oh, that's too many! I'd not have a misunderstanding!"

"I highly doubt my Raven will mistake the gift but I agree it might be hard to explain their source." Phillip crossed his arms. "I'll just wait until all of this business is settled and then pay my debt. How's that?"

Pepper shook her head firmly. "No. It was all a jest. I'm right, of course, but...it was foolish to speak of bonnets. You mustn't!" Her throat tightened and her eyes felt watery and hot without warning.

"Pepper? What is it?"

She pressed her fingertips to her lips.

*What would my darlings think of me if I paraded about suddenly in a bonnet that another man had gotten me?* The twins had been so kind to her lately, stirring her soul with every tender word and compliment. The shame of Southgate haunted her spirits and her growing fear that if they knew... The horror would be compounded if they also thought she was the sort of girl who accepted gifts from men. Jack and Jasper thought her a good girl and her secret adoration of them was too precious to risk.

Not for all the bonnets in the world.

"Prudence?" Phillip asked again.

"Never you mind. I'll be the mistress of my own millinery needs and you just see that you continue to keep out of her sight and clear of the tangle!"

101

"I am a ghost until she sends for me, Pepper."

"Says the man who nearly forfeited all."

"An overdose of honesty I will do my best to avoid in the future," he admitted. "I am who I am, Pepper."

"I like you for it, Sir Warrick. As she loves you for it. Just mind your toes." Pepper stepped back to start to close the door. "Off with you now!"

Phillip smiled as the door's surface missed brushing his nose by the breadth of a few hairs. He was used to the delightful way she abruptly ended every clandestine meeting, the forfeit of civility somehow charming when it was dished out by a tiny strawberry blonde without an ounce of malice in her entire frame.

He stepped back, replaced his topper and made his way down the dark alley, as stealthy as any thief. Raven had banished him and he'd gifted her with the belief that she had the authority to do so. But Phillip Warrick's vows to her the day of his return to London held him fast. He loved her. He'd sworn to never leave her again. Whatever conditions she'd dictated made no difference. Loyalty was embedded in every fiber of his being and Phillip was not some weak soul to cower in ignorance or omit any chance to come to her aid should she need him.

Raven Wells was his.

He'd endured years without her. A few days or weeks without her in his arms and underneath his body were agony but not a torture he couldn't survive.

Phillip sighed. Raven wasn't the only one who had learned to look at the larger board and see the movements of the players. Not that patience was a lesson anyone ever enjoyed. She'd accused him of underestimating her, of not sensing the changes that the events and years had wrought in the girl he'd first kissed in a gazebo. But Phillip accepted that Raven had missed surveying the same in him. She'd become a force in her quest for vengeance but Phillip had also transformed with time and experience.

He was not a man who turned from what he wanted or relinquished his heart's desire—not for scandal, for disaster, nor for self-preservation. If his warrior queen lived for ambushes and the tactics of the battlefield, she'd unknowingly chosen a mate who was built for the strategies of the long siege.

"Billiards." Phillip said quietly as he stepped out onto the street and raised his hand to hail a hackney. "There's a game I understand."

# CHAPTER 12

*T*he play was well attended and Serena did her best to follow the story, pretending indifference to the usual studies from the gallery to the balconies and from the balconies toward each other. Opera glasses were aimed at every portion of the vast space except most notably toward the stage. Not that this was a new phenomenon but tonight it inexplicably grated on her nerves.

Her plans for the evening had unfolded seamlessly.

Well, nearly.

Lord Trent had 'luckily' met them in the lobby, though Adam was missing and Geoffrey had offered no explanation of the change. Harriet had extended an invitation to the earl to join them in their box and the trio had settled in for the evening's entertainments. Lady Lylesforth had deliberately taken a seat between them to diffuse any risk of gossip and Serena had fought not to smile at the miserable show Lord Trent had made of it as he grimly suffered the arrangement.

The end of the first act allowed for a bit of conversation and she marveled at the lump of icy dread she felt. Even so, she turned to her companions with a smile, eyes bright with feigned delight at the prospect of conversation.

"It is very transporting, is it not?" Serena sighed. "I do so love the theatre!"

"Why?" Trent asked in astonishment. "All those wild gestures and ridiculous posturing? My God, I'd rather watch a good fight between fish vendors or those two fat women with the apple cart who insist on screeching on my street each morning."

"Shh!" Harriet snapped her fan shut. "I wonder that you bother to waste your evening then."

"Take it as a grand compliment, Lady Lylesforth. I am questing for any chance to sit in your effervescent and giddy presence." Lord Trent leaned forward with a wolfish grin. "You are irresistible, woman! Give us a taste!"

Serena gasped at the lewd words and knew instantly that he'd gone too far. Harriet hit him so fast that Geoffrey had no defense. It was a smart brutal strike with the rigid baton of her fan across the bridge of his nose and hard enough to probably gift him with a mark in the morning. She was up and out of her seat just as quickly, and Serena shifted to try to offer her friend an arm but Harriet was having none of it.

"Harriet!"

"I need a moment." She was gone through the privacy curtains that covered the door to the upper hall before Serena could restrain her.

"O-of course," Serena said then turned back to assess the damage. Dozens of eyes and magnifying glasses were aimed in their direction at the commotion and she had to force herself to take a slow breath to steady her nerves to return to her seat as if there was nothing out of the ordinary.

The earl yanked out his handkerchief and made a show of pretending to sneeze, all the while clamping down on what might be a broken nose. "God damn it! Women should be forbidden to wield a fan!" He complained under this breath.

"You deserved worse and you know it," she answered him, her expression serene. "Now, sit up and smile or it will be in the papers that the Earl of Trent had his ears publicly boxed by a woman for forgetting his manners."

"It was a harmless jest," he countered as he folded the handkerchief to tuck it away, temporarily satisfied that no blood had been drawn. "Has all humor died in this world?"

Serena sighed. "Not everyone is aware of your keen wit apparently. But that was deliberate. You meant to send her scurrying though I doubt you intended to lose your handsome looks in your scheme."

"You think me handsome, Lady Wellcott?"

"I might have before she added that red stripe to your countenance." She nearly laughed as his vanity immediately altered his expression to one of horror. "I am teasing! Although tomorrow I hope you aren't expected to sit for a portrait when that bruise blooms."

"If I am, I'll pay the artist an extra commission to use a bit of poetic license and omit the worst of it." Lord Trent leaned back in his seat, his own uneven, albeit jovial, nature falling into place. "God, I swear I am still seeing stars! The Widow of Stone packs quite a punch."

A knock at the door prevented her from composing a phrase or two of sympathy as one of the ushers came into the box with a sealed note on a small tray. "Lady Wellcott? There's a message for you, your ladyship."

"Thank you." She retrieved the note, instantly curious but also wary. She had all she wished of surprises and could only pray that Harriet recovered before the intermission was ended.

The usher retreated and Serena eyed the unfamiliar handwriting. It was a firm, elegant hand but one she didn't immediately recognize.

"Receiving love letters in the theatre! How shocking!" Geoffrey teased.

"Do not speak nonsense," she chided as she unfolded the note. "It's more likely a note from someone seeking to ask if you need a doctor."

Lady Wellcott, Forgive me. I am abandoning you to that animal's company but I am too upset to return to the play. I have left the carriage and my footman is to await you and ensure that you make it home safely. I am mortified at my own behavior.

Your sorrowful friend, Harriet.

*Damn, damn, damn.*

*Stay or go?*

She could excuse herself out of concern for Lady Lylesforth and call an end to her evening but a part of her loathed anything that lengthened the game. It was time to start to sprint for the finish. She folded the note and tucked it into her reticule.

*Stay.*

"Was it from Adam?" Trent asked, a small sharp edge betraying his keen interest."

"Adam? Why would your nephew be sending me notes at the theatre?"

His gaze narrowed, a feral creature displeased at the mystery of the message but more angered at his own mistake for bringing up his rival's presence. "He's fool enough. What? Was it some whining apology for missing this chance to fawn at your feet? I certainly hope he didn't fail to mention that he threw you over for some addle-headed codger who wanted him to play with dusty models of dollhouses."

Serena simply looked at him.

"It's true," he added, then crossed his arms. "Who chooses a spotty old man over such company as this?"

The lights began to lower and she sighed. "Your lordship, you are sweet to think that nothing less than the Second Coming should supersede a social outing. I am flattered at the affront you feel on my behalf."

"I think the boy is dazzled by you, Lady Wellcott."

The curtain rose and the lights on stage were lit providing an excuse for her to look away from him. She knew her profile was displayed to every advantage as she answered him, "Is he?"

Geoffrey shifted his weight against one of his chair's arms, attempting to bridge a bit of the space between them thanks to Harriet's vacated seat. "I have come to understand that Adam met you by accident the other day."

"Did he? Where did this happy accident occur?"

"At the museum?"

"Ah, yes! I was taking in the new exhibits and saw him there." She lifted her opera glasses to get a better view of an actress in the throes of a lament. "He has a commendable grasp of art, no doubt because of his studies."

"Adam is not for you."

Her eyes widened and she lowered her glasses to turn toward him. "Pardon me?"

"He is not for you."

"What an odd thing to say! I hadn't thought of him that way but…" She narrowed her gaze. "I know your game. It won't work, Lord Trent."

"What game is that?"

"I know how you work, remember? You think to encourage me by making your nephew seem forbidden." She shook her head. "Ridiculous! I am not a child to be driven to rebellion with such a ham-fisted effort."

"Is it so ridiculous to think you might be attracted to my nephew?"

"He's pretty enough, but—I will be the first to disappoint you. I have no interest in marrying. At least—not…"

"Finish your thought," he commanded.

"I will not. You are a terrible matchmaker, Lord Trent. You always were. Stop pairing me with immature boys." She looked away, as if she'd said too much. "My tastes have changed."

"What are you saying?"

"Nothing." She set her glasses aside completely. "So, Adam is dazzled, is he?" She tipped her head to one side as if reconsidering the notion. "Did he say as much then?"

The earl cleared his throat. "Not one damn word but be that as it may, I meant what I said. My nephew is no match for you, Serena. The boy is the most straight-forward thinker I have ever met. My God, he would bore you after a single meal and…"

She leaned forward and effectively ended his argument with an inadvertent glimpse of the rise of her breasts. "You think I require a man with more wit? With a better view of the game? With a keen mind that can promise me an entertaining life and a variety of diversions?"

He nodded.

"A man with experience of the world who is not afraid of a woman in full possession of her powers? One who has never shied from the limitless pleasure that such a man could provide her?"

His mouth opened a bit, his breath coming a little faster, but he only nodded.

She sighed. "I think you're right, Lord Trent. If only..." Serena stood, unfolding her fan to cool her face as if to ward off the heat of her thoughts. "Forgive me, Lord Trent. I shall leave you to enjoy the rest of the performance. I know how much you loathe feminine weakness."

He stood as well, his expression alight with wary interest. "You are many things but you are not weak, Lady Wellcott."

"I am when it comes to matters of the heart." She took a measured step back, willing herself to imagine that she was starving to death and that Trent was a man constructed entirely out of pastries. The trick must have worked because the heat in his eyes was unmistakable. "We are not strangers. You were once my guardian and it is inappropriate to feel this way about you—the history of our relationship forbids it. We shall not speak of this again. Not ever. Good night, Lord Trent."

She was gone through the curtain and beyond reach before he could climb over the chairs and by the time he was in the hallway, it was impossibly empty. She'd vanished like a ghost.

\* \* \*

"WELCOME HOME, YOUR LADYSHIP." Quinn took her wrap, his expression neutral.

"I'll be working late in the library. I'll have a note or two to go out tonight so please ask one of the men if he would be kind enough to wait for the bell."

"Of course. Would you like Mrs. Holly to send up a tray of refreshments for you while you work?" he offered.

"Yes, that would be lovely." She headed up the stairs and went directly to her small library and study. She delayed changing clothes to get to her desk as quickly as she could. She was a woman on a mission.

Her instincts were jangling in warning at the undercurrent of recent events. Between Mrs. Foxwood's unguarded comments at the card party at Pellbrooks and poor Harriet's unexpected display, she feared she had drawn a bit more attention than she desired from her peers.

Lord Trent's interest was now unmistakable if she gaged it by the emerging heat in Trent's gaze that night. He was snared, perhaps not completely but enough to spur her to take drastic action. Serena began to compose her letters as carefully as a general drafting a tactical plan but the emotional toll slowed her work.

She had only known true love a few times in her life. First, with her adopted parents, a vicar and his wife who had selflessly raised her in an endless shower of affection and praise before their deaths in an epidemic. Then in Phillip's arms, as a young woman coming into her own and dreaming of a life full of passion—a love that had survived the death of dreams. But the third love of her life had been her father, the Duke of Northland. After she'd presented herself to him, he had seen her without judgment and shocked her with his acceptance. The reserve of his title and position had fallen away and he had enfolded her in his generous parental care. The duke had provided all that she needed to rebuild whatever life she desired. And God help her, she had desired to become nothing that resembled her former self. He had given her power, independence and wealth; and she had waited for him to name his price.

But the price had never come.

He had loved her as a father and after the earl's falseness, it had taken her a long time to accept it. But once Serena's heart surrendered to it, the relationship had become almost too precious for the harsh light of day. Her blood relation had provided the social power she needed. Even if the shame of her illegitimacy kept her on the edges of respectability, it had opened doors and allowed Serena to fulfill her ambitions for the Black Rose. But she still guarded her beloved Duke from casual mention and zealously and stubbornly refused to trouble him with the unworthy tangles of her life.

It was an easy choice to justify. If any one of her schemes to secure justice for the women of the Black Rose had unraveled, she wanted to spare him as much damage as she could. It would be a simple matter to distance himself from a by-blow but much harder if he was continually in her sphere or in her company.

Or so she'd told herself until…

Serena laid her pen aside to wrestle with the wave of reluctance and longing that surged through her. She was a woman grown but if her father were there, she feared she would simply curl against him and weep in relief.

She set her papers aside and closed her eyes.

*Now is not the time to go crying to my father or turn into some weak thing seeking for his support or a comforting embrace. But if pride holds me back and stays my hand, will that be consolation enough if it all goes wrong?*

"Pride be damned." Serena opened her eyes and returned to the task at hand, folding and sealing the envelope with a black wax seal and the symbolic impression of a rose. "It is time to roll the dice."

"What was that, your ladyship?" Mr. Quinn asked from the doorway where he held the tray Serena had requested.

"I was nattering to myself again. I apologize."

"A lady should never apologize for thinking aloud," he offered smoothly as he set the tray on the table. "My mother used to say it was only when the empty air answered back that one should consider another approach."

"A good line in the sand to keep in mind but I suspect by the time one has crossed that boundary, they are probably facing greater challenges." She took out another sheet of paper. "Thank you, Quinn."

"You are most welcome."

"This is ready to go out, Quinn. Tell them there's no need to lame a horse but if it can be delivered with good speed, I would be grateful for it."

"Of course. Stanley is anxious to please, your ladyship, and has asked for the task." Mr. Quinn took the note with all the solemnity of a knight accepting a quest. "He is a good man."

"Of course he is." Serena had no fears on that account. Stanley's mother had been a lowly laundress but she had also been one of the first members of the Black Rose's growing ranks and Serena's earliest demonstration that justice would be provided without regard to a woman's rank, or lack of one. When her eldest son had applied for a position in her house, Serena knew that his loyalty would be beyond question. Others in London might worry about the gossip of their household servants, but hers had proven inviolate. "I'll have another but the delivery is within Town."

"Easily managed, your ladyship." Quinn nodded and withdrew to send Stanley on his way to Northland's estates.

Serena's next letter was easier to draft. It was a simple note to reassure Harriet that all was well and that her fan had not caused irrevocable damage either to the earl's nose or to Serena's hopes at large.

She did not add that she suspected that there was more behind Harriet's reaction than mere disgust and affront. It was possible that the dear dowager's heart was ready to return to the land of the living and that the frustrations of a youthful body entombed too quickly were fueling the widow's temper. Not that it was the earl that stirred her, but Harriet was human and perhaps if a better and more thoughtful man dared an approach, Lady Lylesforth's fan would fall to the floor and be forgotten.

She sealed the letter, then finished another note before she rang the bell to summon Quinn when a small quick knock heralded Pepper's entrance.

"I know you're working and prefer not to be bothered," Pepper began as she crossed the room. "But I brought you warm soft slippers and can at least get a few of those hair pins out to let me brush your hair out. It will make you more comfortable for the tasks."

Serena smiled. "You spoil me to a ridiculous degree."

"Well, that's your fault for paying me too much and letting me read romance novels. What kind of friend would I be if I didn't attempt to do what I can in return?" Pepper knelt at her feet and made the exchange of footwear. "Oh, and I wished to tell you that I've word from Fitzherbert's maid."

"Oh? What news from Portman Square?"

Pepper stood and smoothed out her skirts. "Gossip from the neighboring house is that tensions between the earl and his heir are on the rise. There was a bit of shouting though they couldn't determine the specifics. Jenny thought it was a woman they were squabbling about."

"A woman?" Serena repeated softly as she straightened her desk and put away her things. "A tantalizing prospect."

"Won't they just come to blows and be done? Aren't you worried that too much will be said in the heat of an argument between them and they just...reconcile or one of them just yields, tips his hat and says, you're welcome to the lady with my best wishes for your happiness?" Pepper's brow furrowed with her concern. "Gods, this is wrecking my nerves and I ain't even in it!"

"You *aren't* in it," Serena gently amended her friend's speech. "And it is a legitimate worry that the fireworks might take place behind closed doors. But if I know Lord Trent well enough, he loathes direct confrontations. If he is snapping and growling then it speaks volumes of our progress. Sir Tillman will hold his own but he won't have to endure for much longer."

"No?" Pepper became very still, the color in her cheeks deepening. "The season has weeks yet."

Serena stood slowly, shaking her head. "Not for the Earl of Trent."

"My gracious!" Pepper pressed a hand to her heart. "As fast as that?"

"Your ladyship?" Quinn inquired from the doorway.

"Here." Serena held out the notes. "These can go at first light, Mr. Quinn. They are both for addresses within London proper."

Pepper held her tongue until the butler had taken the notes and gone, the door closed behind him. "You've been busy. Most women take to their beds after a bit of theatre, or so I understand."

"I am not, nor have I ever been, *most women*." Serena sighed. "But a few hours of sleep seems a reasonable temptation after the drama of the night."

Pepper accompanied her to her room and assisted her, the ritual of preparations so practiced that neither of them spoke. Serena's thoughts stormed and quieted as she began to measure out each element involved in the days ahead.

She'd openly flirted with a madman.

She had practically announced that she harbored a secret passion for him. If Trent were interested, he would make an open declaration of his own very soon. The conflict with Adam could be over anything —from a differing approach to Oakwell's management, his nephew's refusal to abandon his professional ties or a disagreement about some marital candidate that Trent was shoving under the man's nose.

Or it could be about her.

In any case, she would know the answer soon.

"Tomorrow, I'm taking you to Montpellier's."

"If you insist."

She kissed Pepper on the cheek to wish her good night, retreating to the sanctuary of her bed to wrestle with her schemes. Except that the expanse of sheets and bedding was a cold and empty place and Serena ached to fill it with the raging heat of Phillip's touch and comforting presence.

*Not much longer, my love.*

*So many promises to keep but not much longer.*

*God help me.*

# CHAPTER 13

*T*he billiards room at the Reform Club was one of the most elegantly appointed in the city and popularly enjoyed by its members. The tables were set to allow plenty of space for the players to demonstrate their skills but also for spectators to relax, placing their bets on each round's outcome or making conversation on leather bound chairs set along the edges of the hall. Club referees attended each table officiating the contests while wearing white gloves. A light haze from numerous cigars added to the room's solemnity and masculine aura and as Phillip entered, he took one bracing breath to steel his nerves.

He'd intended to use the wooden score boards the markers were using to locate his man, but found there was no need. Tillman stood out amidst the others, finishing a game at a table across the saloon. Phillip headed over, his steps unhurried and confident.

Sir Tillman's opponent was an older man currently leaning on his cue and theatrically sighing. "What did I do to deserve such a beating?"

Adam smiled. "As bad as that?"

"I am routed out like a schoolboy."

Adam leaned over the table and finished his stroke.

The referee stepped forward. "One hundred, gentleman. The game to Sir Tillman."

"Another, Mr. Simpson?" Adam asked.

"No. I've had my fill, I'm afraid." Mr. Simpson was jovial enough at his surrender.

The timing couldn't have been better as far as Phillip was concerned.

"May I take up the challenge in his stead, sir? The tables are all in play and I was hopeful for an opening to sport a match." Phillip nodded cordially to both men. "Baron Warrick, at your service. Phillip Warrick."

"Then you are welcome," Adam replied. "I am Sir Adam Tillman and this unhappy fellow is Lord Heller."

"I am not always unhappy, Sir Warrick," Peter said his brow tightening. "But how many cannons can one man suffer before he cries off?"

"As bad as that?" Phillip asked.

Adam laughed. "That's what I said only moments ago."

Lord Heller touched his forehead in salute and left them without much more of a farewell and Adam sighed. "God, it's not as if we had bet even a farthing on that match!"

"His pride was worth a bit more to him, I suspect."

"And yours?" Adam asked with a smile. "I'd not invite you to a sulk but I wouldn't mind a fresh opponent if you're willing to risk it."

"The risk is yours." Phillip selected his cue as the referee reset the table. "I haven't linked my pride to contests since I was in short pants."

"Nor have I." Adam nodded as he appeared to take new measure of his acquaintance. "Let's get to it then."

They took their places to determine who would play first, stringing at the referee's signal. Phillip held his breath and then watched in sublime satisfaction as his ball edged out Adam's return to the baulk line. It was by a scant hair's breadth but he didn't care.

*I'm a liar. I'm swimming in pride and jealous rivalry, damn it. Not that billiards is any substitute for much but Hell, I'll take what I can get.*

"You are the striker, Sir Warrick." The referee retrieved the balls to put them in place and then stepped back. "Time or points, gentlemen? What limits do you agree to?"

"Points." Phillip turned to Tillman. "What do you prefer? Two-fifty?"

"Yes. Two-hundred and fifty points should go quickly enough." Adam consented. "Good luck."

"And to you." Phillip turned his attention to the table and began his turn. He was several successful strokes in before he failed to score.

Adam smoothly stepped forward to take his stroke, and the game proceeded, as each man studied the other, immediately aware that they were an equal match and in for a good game. They primarily ignored the referee beyond a scant notice of their progress, their main focus on their opponent.

For Phillip, the challenge was keeping his mind in the room and on the present moment. Adam wasn't making it easy. In another time and place, it rattled Phillip to realize that they would have potentially been good friends. Tillman was his peer in status, age and temperament but it grated against Phillip's nerves to admire anything about the man.

Adam's humor and approach was a sensible foil to his, and they shared the general laments of unmarried titled men in the treacherous waters of society. Phillip avoided giving away any real details of background or history, but Adam was relaxed with his guard down.

*God, if only you had warts or a lisp...I swear I'd be sleeping better at the idea of you dangling for Raven. Then again, how does the love of my life pretending to fawn on a defective ogre make it any better? What a mess!*

"Sir." The referee cleared his throat to politely regain Phillip's focus. "You are in-hand."

"Yes. Yes, of course." Phillip shifted to take his next stroke. "I apologize, Sir Tillman. My thoughts wandered."

"A malady too common to warrant an apology," Adam said. "I'm just grateful you haven't been unkind about my own failings in that area."

Phillip straightened. "I'd have never guessed it. Not by your play." Phillip chalked the leather tip of his cue. "May I ask? I have not met you before at the club. Are you new to London, sir?"

"Not entirely but to these circles, somewhat. I earned my own way as an engineer much to the horror of family. I kept out of the social waters until recently but duty calls."

"That's a trumpet that's hard to ignore."

"I'd complain more but—I'm beginning to accept that rank may have its privileges." Adam's gaze took on a faraway aspect, an interior daydream seizing his imagination. "And London is not without its alluring charms."

"I detect a man on the brink." Phillip said, swallowing the awkward heat of his emotions. "Be careful. The Ton is like a machine that can grind up a dreamer."

"I don't think I'm built for long term survival in London society," Tillman jokingly agreed. "I'm beginning to wonder if there's time yet to make a run for it."

Phillip smiled. "That depends."

"On what?"

"On how many matrons already have you on their short lists and if you have somewhere to hide for the rest of the social season where they can't find you." Phillip said and then fouled his next shot to concede the turn. "Oh, and it also depends on how fast you can run."

"Yorkshire seems to be perceived as the dark side of the moon, so I think I might be safe from pursuit." Adam laughed. "My uncle has referred to it as the jungles of England no less than six times when making introductions."

"Your uncle?" Phillip asked, feigning ignorance.

"The Earl of Trent. Not that I'm attempting to impress you with…" Adam's words trailed off at the remarked change in his new friend's expression. "Are you unwell, Sir Warrick?"

Phillip set his cue down across the table, immediately halting the game. "I concede the game and should say good night. A pleasure meeting you, Sir Tillman."

Adam abandoned his cue over the referee's shocked looks. "Not without a word of explanation, sir."

"G-game to Sir Tillman." The referee stammered.

Phillip looked at the wide eyes of the club attendant and then back at Adam. "Would you care to join me for a brandy in the library, Sir Tillman? It is more private there for conversation."

"Yes. A brandy sounds promising."

The men retreated to the large well-stocked club's library and found a quiet corner to take their seats.

"I am intrigued, Sir Warrick."

Phillip shook his head. "It's not much of a complex mystery. More an awkward admission that I am compelled to share. You seem a very decent fellow, Sir Tillman."

Adam's gaze didn't drop. "Seem? Let's have it, Sir Warrick. Why does the very mention of my uncle end your night?"

"I meant to spare you. The Earl of Trent loathes me and I'm certain that if he discovered that you'd voluntarily spent more than two minutes in my presence, he'd choke the life out of you." Phillip took a casual sip from his brandy. "I have enough on my plate without fearing for your life, sir."

"Why does he hate you?"

"Honestly? When I was twenty-one, I admired a woman he'd bought a bracelet for and in my youthful arrogance, I didn't think he'd mind. I trespassed like the world's stupidest puppy walloping through a mud puddle, tail wagging, and never gave one thought to the mess." Phillip sighed. "I truly believed that male friendship would wink at the mistake but... Lord Trent was not forgiving. He made me pay for it long afterward in ways I never would have anticipated."

"My God, how? Did he call you out?" Adam leaned forward, concern etched into his features.

Phillip waved him off. "The punishment was disproportionate to the crime and I'll not do more damage by rehashing it now. Let's just say that no man holds a grudge longer or with a tighter hold than the Earl of Trent. It is ancient history but I make every effort to avoid the man and didn't realize you were a relation or I would never have approached you for a match. The last thing I desire is the Earl of Trent working himself back up into a frenzy over it and casting back for a fight or fuel for one of his temper tantrums."

"It's been years. Surely the coals have long since died..."

Phillip shook his head. "With anyone else, that would be true. But I know better and logic need not apply to the inner workings of every man."

Adam sat back in his chair. "I did ask you to tell me why. But you are right. Logic is not acquainted with all of us."

"Your first loyalty lies with family. I freely admit I trespassed and was in the wrong with your uncle..." Phillip couldn't help but wince at the wash of remembered pain. "I'd not wish the lesson on any man walking. If by blindly stumbling into you tonight I've caused you any trouble, I hope you'll accept my sincere apologies."

"As bad as that?" Adam asked, then smiled at the echoes of Lord Heller.

Phillip nodded, the humor of it too contagious. "As bad as that."

"Well, it's nothing to do with me and if I see you out and about, I will happily shake your hand, sir," Adam offered as he finished his brandy.

It was Phillip's turn to betray his concerns for his fellow man. "No. As generous as that is, I can't allow that. Protect yourself. And if not for your own safety, then for mine."

"Safety? Uncle Geoffrey can be a handful but I don't think he's a real threat to anyone."

*Oh, God. You're wrong, man. You are so completely wrong.*

Phillip stood abruptly and Adam followed suit.

"I've said my piece. My conscience is clear. I wish you the very best, Sir Tillman. Good night."

"Good night then." Adam held out his hand. "If this is our last meeting, sir, then I hope you'll take it."

Phillip took his hand to shake it, accepting that no matter what else occurred, he would always respect Adam for the gesture. Their grip held, firm and strong, a meeting of equals despite everything between them.

"If you ever need an ally, you may look to me, Sir Tillman. I thank you."

They parted and Phillip didn't look back as he left the club and headed down the broad stairs out onto the street.

* * *

ADAM RETURNED to the brownstone manse on Portman Square, lost in thought.

"Will you need anything else tonight, sir?" the butler asked after taking his coat and hat.

"Where is my uncle?"

"Just returned from the theatre. I believe he is upstairs in his study."

"The theatre?" Adam turned back to give Mr.Walters his full attention. "I forgot the name of the play he'd said he wished to see. What was it again?"

"Fletcher's newest, sir. Something about a Dealing in Duchesses or other."

"Yes, that was it." Adam forced himself to smile. "I think I'll join him for a brandy before I retire, Walters. Thank you."

Adam took the stairs two at a time, reason barely edging out his fury. He strode into the study, unsurprised to find Lord Trent still in his evening clothes, lounging with a glass in his hand and staring at the fire in the fireplace.

"Ah, you're home early!" Trent barely looked up. "Unseasonably cold tonight after that blasted rain today so I'm enjoying a touch of home and hearth. Care to join me?"

Adam poured a small splash of brandy in a cut crystal glass. "How was the play?"

Trent rolled his eyes. "You aren't going to pout about it, are you?"

"You told me that you had plans to see an ailing friend and that I should amuse myself somewhere." Adam crossed to take the chair across from the man. "Why would you lie?"

"Can't a man desire a night off from babysitting?" Uncle Geoffrey sat up a touch straighter, vaguely defensive. "The play was wretched and I spared you hours of boredom so be sure to remember to thank me at some point."

"And how was Lady Wellcott? Did you see her there?"

It was a guess. A childish guess but he made it all the same and was rewarded with the guilty smirk on his uncle's face.

"I ran into her and her horrible chaperone by sheer chance as Providence would have it." Geoffrey took a sip from his brandy. "Lady Wellcott flourishes and thrives, especially when she can bask in the glow of my attention without your tree-like shadow blocking her view."

*Shit.*

"How lovely for her." Adam leaned forward, his gaze narrowing to make sure the flickering firelight wasn't playing tricks on his vision. "What happened to your nose?"

Lord Trent's hand flew to cover his nose, his color deepening in fury. "Nothing! Nothing of consequence!"

Adam smiled. He'd taken a blow of some kind across the bridge and if Adam were a gambling man, it was likely from Lady Serena Wellcott putting him in his place.

*Thank God.*

Adam leaned back and stretched out his legs, deliberately making a show of his own contentment. "Well, if it's nothing…"

"I had a *glorious* time."

"How very nice for you." Adam took a sip from his glass and watched the fire.

Geoffrey shifted in his chair, fighting a sulk. "Actually, I am not exaggerating. It was quite an enlightening evening."

"Hmm." Adam's reaction was that of a man being told a stranger's shoe size or preference for butter or jam. If he wanted to get to the bottom of things and achieve his goals, he knew better than to beg for details. Adam allowed the quiet crackle of the fire to work its magic.

"What are you thinking of over there? I say I have an *enlightening* evening in the company of the most beautiful woman in England and you—you say 'hmm'?!"

"I would rather not tell you what I'm thinking since you are already angered over God knows what over there when any other man would be giggling with glee if your claim were true." Adam shrugged his shoulders and took another sip of his drink. "You are a puzzle, sir."

"You'll tell me. I'll have it!"

"Very well." Adam set his glass down. "I was thinking that Lady Wellcott has never struck me as a woman who would be interested in a man who lacked self-confidence. Oh, well, women are a mystery!"

"What? I care nothing for the woman's interests but I have no shortage of confidence."

Adam smiled and shook his head. "Of course, you don't. That's why you lied about your plans and made sure I wasn't in attendance. You've gotten it stuck in your head that you cannot take me in a head-to-head rivalry and that if I am there, you have not a sliver of sunlight's chance in Hades with the lady."

"That's ridiculous!"

"Naturally. But the Tree is flattered all the same." Adam yawned.

"She is not interested in you, not even vaguely interested."

Adam said nothing, but continued to look at Lord Trent as one would a babbling infant.

"Damn it," Geoffrey continued, over enunciating each word as his fury increased. "She told me in plain speech that you are not in the running!"

Adam smiled. "How convenient and yet you stable me all the same. Don't overwork yourself, dear uncle. Next time you bid me to go out to call on friends, I will go without a backward glance. I am frankly happy to allow you to sabotage yourself with these childish ploys. I think it is sweet the way you strive to win her. Though if you need to remove every man who is younger or taller than you are from her sight, you are in for an uphill battle. London's population is going to prove a challenge."

"Watch your words, boy!"

Adam sighed. "I apologize. In my defense, you asked."

"You think I see you as a rival? You are my match in nothing! I shall haul you along and tie you to my hip for the rest of the season and you will regret your challenge, stupid whelp! You look like a pie vendor standing next to me, Adam. You're oblivious to the snickering laughter and rude comments made behind your back, but I am not. I hear all of it and the talk is that the comedy of seeing you 'play earl' is much anticipated. But you think by inserting yourself into her presence with me as a foil that you won't look even more ridiculous? You're a fool!" Geoffrey's grip on his glass tightened until his knuckles shown white. "But let's have it unfold, shall we? And slowly. Why rush humiliation, Adam, when it will be all the more rich when I dish it to you in teaspoons!"

"As you wish." Adam stood slowly and made his way from the room. "Good night then, Uncle Geoffrey. And, before I forget," he hesitated in the doorway for just a moment. "Thank you for sparing me from hours of boredom."

Adam closed the door just as Trent's crystal glass shattered into a thousand pieces against it. It was a dangerous move but he'd decided to take Sir Phillip Warrick's advice to heart.

But he would do it by keeping the wolverine on a leash and close at hand.

# CHAPTER 14

*T*he morning was grey and damp but the gloom never touched Serena's buoyant mood. She had received noted from two different sources reconfirming that Lord Trent and his nephew were at odds. Or more accurately, that the earl was in a public sulk and at odds with himself. Descriptions of Adam Tillman conveyed that he was congenial and civil despite the erratic temper of Lord Trent. "This bit about my fortunes being a fiction is my favorite part."

"God, the man is daft! Where in the world is he getting that foolishness?" Pepper asked as she finished arranging Serena's hair.

"What does it matter? I am poor, am I?" Serena said with a smile. "How crafty of me to disguise it so brilliantly!"

Pepper rolled her eyes. "Three houses, that stone keep in the north and vaults of money you don't have years enough on this earth to spend. Oh, you're disguising it so well I think I should give you alms, poor thing!"

"Come, Pepper. Madame Montellier sent word that my newest ballgown is ready. I wish to pick it up personally this morning and then see if we cannot get you a new dress or two."

Pepper shook her head. "You're too generous! I am happy to go with you without the promise of a dress. A few yards of cloth or even a cast off or two from any closet within your reach, and I'd still be the best dressed maid in all of London!"

"Indulge me."

"I am not in need of a new gown, Lady Wellcott." Pepper tried to dig in her heels. "I've no room in my trunk for another."

"Then give your old ones away to Molly. She adores a new dress. Come." Serena stood from the dressing table and sailed out without looking back, completely confident in Pepper's obedience, even if it were reluctantly given in her current mood. "I'll tell Quinn we need the carriage."

Within the half hour, they'd arrived at the dressmaker's and Pepper accompanied her to the fitting room. Pauline brought the ball gown for inspection and Serena sighed with delight, reverently lifting the detailed sleeve to admire the work. "It is a dream and so...fitting. What do you think, Pepper?"

"I think it's the prettiest thing I've ever seen."

"Please box it for transport home, Madame Montellier. And here," she held out a folded note. "Some news for your most talkative clients to accidentally overhear."

Madame Montellier nodded with a knowing smile. "The best rumors are the stories one isn't meant to know."

"I rely on you, Pauline."

"Was there anything else?"

"If you would allow us some privacy, please."

Pauline nodded and held out the key with its black satin ribbon. "Of course, your ladyship."

Once they were alone, Pepper held aside the curtain covering the hidden door and then slipped inside after her to the parlor. As Serena lit the lamp, Pepper made a quick assessment of the room's state. "I shall bring dried flowers to freshen the air a bit."

"It is not meant for elegance."

Pepper wrinkled her nose. "I should say not."

Serena paid her complaints very little attention. Pepper's opinion of the state of the Black Rose's secret parlor was not new to Serena's hearing. She pulled the heavy brocade back and the twins quickly stepped inside.

"Morning, your ladyship," Jasper said then both men looked at Pepper. "Good morning, Miss Prudence," they intoned in unison.

Pepper blushed. "Good morning."

"It's a...bit of sunshine on such a day to see you, Pepper." Jack bit his lower lip. "Is that a new frock?"

Jasper's brow furrowed. "Don't be daft. It isn't new, is it? She wore it last week but with the yellow wrap, yes?"

Pepper's blush deepened in color. "I wonder that you'd remember it."

Jack was not going to be out done. "Of course, she did. And the bonnet with the blue ribbons. We enjoy the sight of you, Pepper."

"We do." Jasper nodded. "We do, indeed."

Serena cleared her throat, subtly reminding them that she was yet in the room. "Pepper, if you don't mind, why don't you go back into the fitting room, ring for Madame Montellier and choose two day dresses for yourself? If the twins can recall every dress you own, then I believe I've won our earlier argument. I'll be out to join you in just a few minutes."

"Yes. As you wish," Pepper said, retreating after rewarding each of the men with a quick shy smile.

Once the door was closed behind her, Serena watched in amusement as the men did their best to recover their wits.

"Sorry, your ladyship. We..." Jack began.

"...forgot our manners." Jasper finished. "You look very nice, as well."

"Dear God," Serena sighed. "No fear, gentlemen. My vanity is intact and unfazed. I did mean to thank you for coming on such short notice and alert you to a shift in our timeline. We have days, not weeks and I need you to do something for me."

They looked at her, loyalty and obedience glowing in their eyes. "You have but to say it, your ladyship."

She invited them to sit at the table and Serena carefully and calmly outlined her plans.

"In the event of my death, here is what you will do…"

LATER THAT AFTERNOON, Serena made a round of social calls in a deliberate show of normalcy. She deflected questions regarding Trent, instead turning conversations back toward a friend's search for a lady's maid, upcoming balls or the matchmaking prospects of the newest batch of debutantes. Today, she was Lady Serena Wellcott, respectably shocked at any hint of gossip, the sweetest version of a woman averse to all conflict and vice.

It was in Lady Hodge-Clarence's sitting room she faced the last hurdle.

"I must say, Lady Wellcott, it is hard not to speculate on the Earl of Trent's intentions toward you. He appears so often in your company!"

Serena smiled, but shook her head. "He is in London to introduce his nephew to his peers. His intentions are fairly harmless, I think. He has asked repeatedly if I will act as an aide to him by offering an opinion on the eligibility of the various women seeking Sir Tillman's attention. As a friend, he is aware of my connections in Town and knowledge of the best families."

Ursula nodded. "I see. So it is merely as an advisor that he seeks you out?"

"Just so." Serena refolded her hands in her lap. "Naturally, I am happy to offer what help I can but…"

"You have reservations?"

"At the end of it all, I am perhaps too soft-hearted for the task. For even when I know a young lady may not be entirely suited, it is too crushing to say something unkind and I hesitate to do so!" Serena sighed. "I should defer to a stronger soul like yourself, Lady Hodge-Clarence. The earl would be better served, and Sir Tillman as well."

"Oh, I am flattered to hear you say it!" Ursula puffed up immediately. "You are wise beyond your years to recognize your limitations. Youth makes a cautious sage. He is foolish to have placed that burden on your shoulders and then expose you to ridiculous gossip as a result."

"Then I am glad you braved the topic, your ladyship. I will direct Lord Trent to seek a more experienced hand and I shall be more mindful of appearances." Serena made a subtle glance at the mantle clock to gage the time. A proper social call was a brief thing, choreographed and balanced. "He is so much older than I am, Ursula, that it never occurred to me that anyone would think…well, the unthinkable. But after Mrs. Foxwood uttered—" Serena pressed her gloved fingertips against her lips, standing. "I am determined to rise above it, Lady Hodge-Clarence, and I will ignore all vile hints to the contrary until the danger has passed."

Ursula stood as well, the cold flint in her eyes flashing with approval. "It is your only option."

"Thank you, Lady Hodge-Clarence. It was such a pleasure to see you today. Do give Mrs. Foxwood my best regards."

"I shall. Good-bye, Lady Wellcott."

Serena sailed out, satisfied at the outcome. Directing or fueling gossip of any kind was more of an art than a science. She'd long waged a campaign of misdirection when it came to herself, cautiously bolstering the stories that worked to her advantage and enlisting members of the Black Rose to squash any tales that didn't.

But with her current mission, it was critical to keep opinion divided. There must be enough speculation to encourage Trent to believe in his growing chances with her but also a solid camp of those who would surround and support her innocence when the critical moment came.

On the carriage ride home, it was Phillip who dominated her thoughts.

She'd expected to miss him but the sensation had grown into a raw, gnawing ache that ate away at her equilibrium. Nearly two weeks without him and she was miserable beyond words.

*Ridiculous. It is temporary and fleeting, this separation, and moaning after him like a child accomplishes nothing!*

The rigors of self-discipline proved useless. It was as if once reconciled to Phillip, her soul had finally slipped its bounds, stubbornly setting onto happiness and ignoring her bid to carry on without him.

Ruthless denial yielded no relief. Love bared its teeth and Serena marveled that anyone didn't crumble at this force.

Finally, the carriage stopped at her town home and Serena climbed down with her footman's assistance. As she crossed the threshold, she was all business. "Quinn, I am in for the rest of the day and accepting no callers."

"A letter came for you, your ladyship. I mention it only because Miss Prudence indicated that you would wish to be instantly alerted to the fact." Quinn held out the small silver tray with the day's correspondence, the letter on top of the small pile seizing her attention.

"Yes. Quite right." Serena took only the letter, leaving the rest, and retreated without a word to her upstairs study and sitting room. She closed the door behind her and then opened the sealed message from Delilah Osborne, the newest member of the Black Rose.

Dear Lady Wellcott, I wished to send you word before the formal notice is put into the papers and the obituary is composed. I have received word from America that James unexpectedly died on the voyage from a terrible infection and fever. He was buried at sea. I have made a vague claim that Southgate holds too many painful memories and have made plans to mourn privately, though unconventionally, by taking a journey to the Continent where my health and the health of my child may fare better. Dell and I are away by month's end. I shall send word upon our return and hope this note finds you happy.

Yours in Eternal Gratitude,

Delilah Osborne

Serena read the note through three times before she put it down on her desk. She admired Delilah's restraint and phrasing, aware that if the letter had fallen into the wrong hands, there was no hint of the Black Rose's hand in it or their conspiracy to protect the future heir to Southgate.

James was dead.

Serena waited in the quiet. She waited for remorse, or regret; curious to see if anything would emerge beyond the sleek satisfaction of knowing that the world had shed itself of one more useless predator. She waited for any hint of guilt at her part in James' demise and encountered—nothing.

And then the wave hit.

Her hands trembled, the paper in her hands crumpling into a twisted mass with the force of it. For what did it mean when she could feel nothing? Usually with triumph came joy—dark insidiously seductive joy at her accomplishments. It was as addictive as any opiate and the fuel she had survived on for nearly seven years.

*I should feel something! Glee? Satisfaction? Amusement? Fear? Grief? Repugnance?*

But there was nothing. It was a black void at her feet that threatened her in infinite ways she had never anticipated.

James Osborne, the rapist, was dead from the poison of his injured and rotting genitals and she alone had engineered the possibility. If it wasn't murder, it was an angel's sigh from it.

And she felt nothing.

*Oh, God. Have I crossed some irrevocable line? Lost my humanity and—*

Serena lifted her head, annoyed at a foreign sound that interrupted her struggles. A strange keening sound that cut through her terror until she realized that she, herself, was the source of it.

She was on her feet, panic's grip icy and cruel against her throat.

Serena battled to hold her own, to simply rein in the alien fear and numb horror of at once being out of control and the humiliation of powerless emotion.

*Lost.*

*I am lost, at last.*

But then, impossibly, Phillip was there. His arms around her, the warmth of his body, the strength of his hold pressing her to the wall of his chest, to the rhythm of his heart and he was raining kisses on her tear-streaked face. Long minutes passed as he lifted her into his arms, carried her to the sofa and simply held her until the storm began to pass. "There, there, my dearest. Don't cry."

"I am not...crying...am I?" Serena whispered, the world tilting to encompass Phillip Warrick and nothing else. "I never cry."

"Of course, you don't," he said softly and kissed her forehead. "How foolish of me."

Her arms reached up to caress his back, drinking in the tender touch of his lips to her skin. "How did you know to come? How is this possible?"

"Delilah sent me word of James' passing and I came on impulse as soon as I read her note. She said she'd sent you the same news and I feared for you."

"Why?" She looked up at him, eagerly inventorying his face, immediately strengthened by the familiarity of every line, by the color of his eyes, by the support she read there. "Why when I neglected to fear for myself?"

He shook his head. "You never fear for yourself, Raven."

"I am a monster, at last. James. I..." Her fingers tightened their hold on him. "I am not sorry. Do you hear me? I am not sorry in the least."

"You mustn't punish yourself this way. Did you truly hope to shed a tear over that animal?" Phillip asked. "Hell, I'm hard pressed to think of a person who might so much as blow their nose when the announcement is made."

"No. Not tears but—usually there is...something. But when I read the note and there was *nothing*," Serena's voice broke as her throat threatened to close up again before she managed to go on. "It surprised me."

"You are allowed to be in shock. Anticipating someone's fall is different than the reality." Phillip stroked her hair, tenderly drawing his fingers down the side of her bare neck. "You've never had a man drop dead in your wake, dearest. It's bound to be a shock."

She smiled, the first solid sign that she was fully recovering her wits. "You think him the first? How sweet of you, Sir Warrick."

"Shh! If there's a platoon of bodies under the hedges in your garden now is not the time to discuss them." He smiled as he lowered his mouth to hers. "I love you, Raven."

"Even now?"

"Even now. Stop talking." He kissed her but then strayed from her mouth, trailing soft teasing fire along the line of her jaw, upward to the curve of her ear. He playfully sampled her earlobe sending shivers down her spine. The fichu he dispensed with easily, loathing any bit of frippery that kept her flesh from his easy touch.

"Oh! How is it possible that you…can do that so easily?" she sighed.

He lifted his head. "Do what?"

In answer, she rewarded him with the last thing he ever expected. The lady blushed, a delicate pink crept up her cheeks and Phillip was rocked at the sight.

"Is the lady aroused?" he asked softly.

"The lady is—most assuredly aroused."

"Then we must see to that."

Serena sighed and tipped her face up for his kiss. She felt ridiculously cautious after her outburst but then strangely fearless as he folded her into his embrace. Phillip was her comfort, her rock and her anchor to the version of herself she liked best.

His kiss was not so much a thing that feasted on her touch, but it felt more like a renewal of her spirit. Every pass of his mouth across hers, every taste, resuscitated her will and longing to heal. Serena sighed for more and without a word, he stood to take her hand and led her down the hallway to her bedroom.

He did not kick down the door but she didn't wish for more than the gentle command of his hand holding hers. He locked the door behind them and Serena smiled at the gesture.

*There's not a servant in this house who will put one foot on the tread of those stairs until Pepper signals them that it is permissible. But it is endearing that he guards my modesty—even now.*

There was no rush to the exchange. He undressed himself and watched as she did the same, gracefully making a dance of the removal of each layer. For ties and stays, he became her assistant, willfully using his tongue to trace patterns across her sensitive flesh to pebble her skin with the teasing caress of his breath over each moist line. She leaned against him, shivering, and Phillip pushed the last of her clothes onto the floor.

At last, she was naked before him, shameless and evocative.

And vulnerable.

It was a new trait for her but his throat closed at the bare ghostly hint of it in her eyes. Phillip stepped close to her until they were heartbeat to heartbeat, face to face, like mirrors of each other with their breath intermingling. He waited until there was nothing but a calming heat between them.

Serena tried to guess what he meant, even as her spirits responded to the healing quiet. She'd expected an erotic rush to distract her from the strange agonies of the afternoon, but Phillip just held her.

*God, how had I ever thought to push him away?*

# CHAPTER 15

"*Y*es?" he asked softly.

"Yes."

He bent over to kiss the rise of her breasts, lingering over each to weight them in his hands, kiss the sensitive curves and even to tongue the crease underneath where she imagined she had never been touched. He paid homage to every inch, then suckled at the taut peaks of her breasts until her knees melted at the storm of longing he evoked.

She started to kneel, thinking to repay the favor and demonstrate again that she know how to please him best but Phillip held her up with a smile, his grip gentle on her arms. He shook his head and wordlessly guided her up onto the bed, arranging her at its center to lie by her side.

He kissed her but this time, it was like coming home. She could taste his need and willed him to know hers. Phillip met her every move, countering each change in her mood as smoothly as a maestro bringing a living instrument into tune.

She reached down to seize his sex, determined to guide him inside of her, unwilling to wait but he evaded her touch by capturing her wrists and drawing them up above her head.

"Raven."

"I need you to ride me until I'm senseless, Warrick. I need—I need you to make me cry," she whispered.

He slowly shook his head.

"I need to feel, Phillip."

"I know, my dearest. But not through pain. No more pain today. Come back to me, let me bring you back to me."

He slid his hand down over her belly, through the dark damp curls above her folds and found what he sought. She bucked her hips upward against his hand, her thighs parting to demand more of his touch, as if to dictate the tenor of the intrusion and lure him into roughly pressing into her, into giving her the ruthless friction she wished. But Phillip refused and instead began the lightest assault, feather soft and tender until his fingertips were coated in the slick honey of her body. He found her clit and danced over the pearl in a circular dance, even as he kissed her throat again and renewed his efforts to win her.

She resisted him at first. The slow gentle pace of his touches, the soft slide of his kisses over her skin—here was the most tender assault that didn't allow her to silence her thoughts or numb herself to what had happened. He forced her to be present, to be still, and to allow him to simply love her.

"Faster. Harder." Serena begged him then bit her lip at the alien sound of her own pleas.

"Shh. Wait for it, sweetling. There. Yes?"

God help her, yes! Frustration yielded to the undeniable truth that her body was not complaining of pace, pressure or the philosophy of Phillip Warrick's approach. She'd habitually expected a rush to her own releases, familiar with the healthy pattern of her desires but this —this was new. Slow and steady was not only winning the race but it was redefining where the finish line might be...

He kept kissing her while his free hand roamed to cup her breasts, pinching and caressing them in turn to heighten her anticipation. But the fingers at her clit never stopped dancing a slow minuet against her flesh—they never shifted pace. Instead her heart began to thrum and pulse to the rhythm he dictated and once they matched up, a chasm of bliss opened at her feet.

She began to come in a molasses fall of ecstasy that mercilessly stripped her of reason. The climax's grip was so total that Serena feared she would come apart in his arms. She cried out, a mindless keening song of joy that transported her from herself. It was all she could manage to cling to him and pray that she hadn't bloodied him too badly when she realized that her fingernails had dug into his back.

"Oh, God. That was...impossible!" she sighed. "A bit selfish of me, don't you think?"

"It's not a race, dearest." Phillip shifted up onto his elbow. "But since you've so generously offered..."

"W-what did I offer?"

He was up in a flash, moving her easily into position. Her resistance was a mirage, her body still shuddering from the after-effects of an orgasm she had yet to overcome. Phillip moved behind her and Serena gasped at the discovery of kneeling to be pushed over onto her elbows, a wicked offering for her lover.

The tip of his cock was molten hot and so large against her sensitive flesh that Serena squeaked in surprise but a lustful part of her began to keen again, as if the raw hunger could accept nothing less than this—than all of him.

She deliberately lifted her hips to align her body to his and readied for his thrust. It came fast and hard, her channel tighter than tight as the angle gave him the deepest access to her inner core. He filled her completely, so perfectly, she nearly wept but his withdrawal came just as quickly and Serena threw her head back to revel in the sensations.

The line between conquest and surrender blurred and was lost.

Serena took and gave, her world defined by Phillip's cock pounding into her body, by the greedy tug of her slick channel desperately trying to hold him, by friction and thrust, by everything that connected him in a new feverish dance that neither one of them could stop.

She sat up, so that with every stroke, they moved together. Phillip was lifting her up, gripping her hips, then cupping her breasts, encircling her in his arms until her cries intensified and he knew he might have taken her too far, but he couldn't turn back. His own need for release was too powerful.

His body tightened in a molten pitch of tension before he climaxed at last, as if electrical arcs were firing up his spine, and he jetted inside of her with a cry of his own. He was grateful that she was facing away from him, for he feared his grimace of pleasure was not exactly his best expression.

Though truly...vanity was not high on his mental list of priorities.

*But if I burst into tears—God, let me keep a small shred of dignity, please.*


Serena dropped her head, resting back onto her elbows and accidentally sending another wave of shuddering stimulation up his frame.

Phillip instantly gripped her hips to still her with a playful growl. "Don't. Move."

She laughed. "As you wish."

He took a few slow and careful breaths before he could extricate himself without crying out. "Dear mother of heaven—that was...a much better way to spend an afternoon."

She rolled on her back, a sensuous siren looking up at him in open admiration. "What are you thinking at this moment? I am curious."

"I am thinking that I will never again forfeit days or nights in your company. If I have the choice, of course." He added the last to appease her but a satisfied voice in side of him was crowing endlessly. She was *his*. No matter what games or schemes swirled around them, no matter how many times she bid him to "stand aside", she was marked for his, in ways that only they understood.

"Of course."

"Better?"

"Nearly." Serena sighed with contentment. "I am restored enough to be mortified at that scene."

He lay back down next to her, stroking the black silken curls from her face. "You are human, Raven. Remember?"

"Yes. That was what frightened me. For a few moments, I feared I wasn't anymore." She shuddered. "It is a sensation I have no desire to repeat."

"Are you abandoning your course?" he asked softly.

"No." Serena shifted to sit up in bed, not bothering with the modesty of bedding as she faced him. "I want it over and done. It is the anticipation and delay taking its toll on my nerves. I am sure of that now."

"How close is it?"

"I don't know. I hope to drive him to ground before the end of the month."

"And Tillman?"

Serena smiled. "Still jealous?"

Phillip nodded. "Naturally. But I don't wish the man harm."

"Nor do I." Serena leaned over to kiss him, "Bed me, Phillip. Make me feel everything again."

"As my lady wishes."

He covered her with his body, conqueror and keeper, protector and slave. He was a warm shield from all that was pain and Serena sighed in contentment and drank in the healing balm of Sir Phillip Warrick's passion and at last, of his trust.

# CHAPTER 16

*L*ady Lylesforth walked alongside Serena on the public garden's wide graveled path, the pair taking a respectable stroll to savor the mild weather of the day. Serena was glad for the company and the opportunity to reassure her Dragon that all was well. Harriet's confrontation with Trent had rattled her nerves more than she was willing to admit and Serena deliberately did not bring up the earl in their conversation.

She shifted her parasol to take advantage of its pretty interior at showing off her bonnet and face, and sighed.

"You are preening over there, Lady Wellcott."

"I am." Serena smiled. "You should try it, Lady Lylesforth. Someone once told me that nothing was more becoming on a woman than well-applied vanity."

"What a preposterous thing to say! Who told you that?"

Serena's pleasure in the morning faltered. *Trent. Trent said that. My God, and I just quoted him like a giddy idiot.* "I meant it as a jest. I apologize. For some reason I am in a nonsensical mood today."

"No. What a dreary and somber character I've become! I marvel at it sometimes, Lady Wellcott. I barely recognize this Widow of Stone, striking men in the face and huffing about every little thing."

"I like you in any guise, Harriet. You are a good friend. I'm sure it will come to you that you can be any version of yourself that you wish to be. It is the most transforming power in the world, Lady Lylesforth."

"You say that as if a woman need merely pronounce herself to be a bird and then express what color she wishes her feathers to be!" Harriet laughed.

Serena smiled. "Precisely. Now you are beginning to see the way of it." She jauntily twirled her parasol. "Today, I am a peacock, Lady Lylesforth."

Harriet glanced down at her dark skirts, black gloves and matching parasol. "I remain a crow."

"For now."

"Are you enjoying the season so far, Lady Wellcott?"

Serena shook her head. "I don't think pleasure is one of my goals, but I am trying to take hold of what happiness I can. I live in hope, Harriet, that I can accomplish for myself what I do for others; but beyond the next few days, my knowledge of my future is as murky as a bog."

"Life affords so few opportunities for joy. I marvel that you still possess any hope at all. You take on so many other women's troubles and heartaches, Lady Wellcott. How are you not crushed under the weight of it all?"

"Goodness, you *are* melancholy this morning," Serena sighed. "May I remind you that the Black Rose Reading Society is dedicated to improving the lives of its members? I carry nothing. I do what I can and I move on. I have no dissatisfied customers as of yet and if anyone wishes to lodge a complaint, I defer them to the twins. Though after this outing, I wonder if I should send them your way. Harriet? What in the world is driving this?"

"I don't know. I am...restless." Harriet stiffened her spine. "Never mind. It is nothing a turn through the park cannot cure and *nothing* I cannot manage by simply ignoring it."

Serena smiled. "How very English of you!"

They walked on, nodding and exchanging greetings with acquaintances as they passed.

"Oh, heavens!" Harriet said under her breath. "Has she seen us? It's too late to run now."

Lady Pringley came up the path toward them, a ridiculous amount of dyed ostrich plumage bobbing with each step, her maid hobbling behind her with a large basket. "Ladies! What a pure delight!"

"Lady Pringley!" Serena stepped forward as if eager for the meeting, a smile on her face. "You are a vision of beauty, dear Beatrice."

"What is that color you are wearing? Is that lilac?"

"Hyacinth," Serena supplied. "It is a shade of purple perfected by my couturier, Madam Montellier. She has a delightful establishment near Haymarket."

"I shall descend upon her and see if I cannot steal her from you, Lady Wellcott." Lady Pringley announced her intentions with the confidence of a pirate. "Ah, Lady Lylesforth. I had heard that you were shepherding Lady Wellcott this season but I could scarcely credit the news. All my invitations to do the same these last few years came to naught and I was convinced that you were going to wall yourself up in a castle somewhere like a gothic hermit."

Harriet shook her head. "Alas, the masons in Dorset convey that they are working as quickly as they can to seal off a keep but my retreat is not yet finished. I am forced to remain amidst society for a while longer."

Lady Pringley blinked in surprise as Harriet went on. "Lady Wellcott's offer was for a companion and chaperone. I knew she had no hidden aims to arrange my next marriage or ambush me with introductions to eligible men. Whereas I'm afraid I did not have the same confidence with your invitations, Beatrice. I hope you'll forgive me."

"I might," Lady Pringley stated. "If you at least concede to participating in my croquet tournament next month. Both of you *must* come! And what's more..." Lady Pringley's complete attention shifted to Serena's face. "What is this?"

"Whatever do you mean, Lady Pringley?"

"You are positively glowing with some inner secret over there, your ladyship! Can it be that the elusive Lady Wellcott is at long last in love?" Lady Pringley pivoted like a hunter seeking prey. "Did you just spot the man in question? Is that why your color ripened so?"

"Beatrice!" Serena exclaimed then dropped her chin, to look at the woman through her lashes. "You are too discerning!"

Harriet gasped. "What?"

Lady Pringley's expression became one of rapt triumph and raw hunger for the delicious promise of secrets spilled and fresh gossip. "Are you truly in love, Lady Wellcott?"

Serena took a deep breath and ignored Harriet's open shock and disbelief. "I may well be."

"Of course you are! I knew it." Lady Pringley crowed. "I can spot a woman in the throes of an attachment from a hundred paces."

Harriet pressed her lips together so tightly they lost all color. "What a remarkable talent."

"Who is the lucky gentleman who has captured your fancy?" Lady Pringley pressed. "You must tell me! I am the soul of discretion!"

*You are the soul of wagging tongues and provocative tales, you old bat. But what an easy game you make of it!*

"I cannot say. He has not declared his feelings and I am mortified that I have blurted out my own state or that it is so evident in a single glance." Serena pressed one gloved hand to her cheek as if to force the color to retreat. "I trust you to keep my confession to yourself. Please, Beatrice."

"Of course, of course, I will." Lady Pringley's eyes shone with excitement to be off with her news. "Come, Dierdre," she said to her maid. "We must make haste if we are to arrive at our next appointment on time."

"Yes, your ladyship," Dierdre said without lifting her eyes from the basket.

"Farewell, Lady Lylesforth and Lady Wellcott. Do enjoy your stroll!"

Pringley hurried off, her maid a forlorn tail.

"Are you mad? She'll have it all over London before breakfast tomorrow!"

"What will she have all over London?"

"That—That you are in love with…" Harriet's brow tightened in frustration. "Someone!"

Serena smiled and then elegantly shrugged her. "A vague bit of news to get so excited over, do you not agree?"

"It is too vague by miles." Harriet closed her parasol as they continued on their way. "My God, that woman will conjecture the worst and name a dozen different possibilities! It is a nightmare!"

"It is a silly squall that will excite only those who hold a stake in the race."

"To expose yourself to speculation? You have no control over the direction it will take. It is madness. My God, they may even say that it is the *Earl of Trent* who has ensnared you!" Harriet shuddered.

Serena playfully winked at her friend. "Oh, my! What an imagination you have…"

Harriet's steps stuttered to a halt. "You terrify me sometimes."

"Only sometimes?" Serena asked. "I am losing my touch."

# CHAPTER 17

*T*he next day, Serena awoke before dawn to manage the critical correspondence of the day and to redraft a letter to her solicitor. She was determined to leave no loose ends and worked through the morning. Never before had she been so personally tangled in a scheme and Serena knew that nothing blinded faster than emotions. She'd wielded the weapon against others but this time the blade was in her own hands.

Milbank's masque ball was five days off. It was the social height of the season and word had it everyone who was anyone would be in attendance. Not that they would publicly flaunt their invitations. It was an infamous event for liaisons made and scandals gilt in sin, so naturally no one ever missed it.

*It is perfect. Time to fan the flames and ensure that even if Lord Trent has reservations for---*

A knock on the door interrupted her thoughts.

"Come in."

Quinn entered, and she instantly knew he was displeased. "It is barely ten and far too early for a social call, your ladyship."

"Who is it, Quinn?"

"The Earl of Trent has presented himself at our doorstep, your ladyship. He has stubbornly refused to leave and insisted that he'll wait while you…" Quinn had to swallow his distaste before finishing, "get out of bed and dress yourself."

Serena nodded. Quinn was insulted on her behalf and there was no need to acknowledge the affront. Her skin felt cold but she kept still. "Put him in the first floor sitting room and have him wait there. Ask Albert to stand ready. Alert Pepper that I have a caller and ask Mrs. Holly to see that we have something on hand should the earl require refreshments."

"Very good, your ladyship." Quinn retreated to carry out her orders and Serena carefully put away all her papers, refusing to rush.

*Damn it. If he kneels on my carpet and declares himself privately, all is lost.*

When everything was put away, she stood slowly to survey herself in a mirror on the wall. Her green silk morning dress was pretty enough, but suddenly she wasn't sure what gown or accessory would be appropriate for Trent's unexpected call.

As she descended the staircase, she composed her strategy and by the time she crossed the parlor's threshold, she was set. She left the door open behind her, nodding to Albert to hold his place in the hall where he could discreetly hear all should events take a turn.

"Lord Trent. To what do I owe the dubious honor of a morning call?"

"Why wait to pay a woman compliments? Who determined such a thing had to be held off until well after luncheon?" Geoffrey smiled. "It's ridiculous if you consider it."

"I like the formalities that we impose on ourselves, Lord Trent." She crossed the room, inviting him to take his place on the settee while she selected an armed chair on the opposite side of the arrangement. "But what brings you here? It surely isn't the clumsy excuse of paying me compliments. Is there news of some kind? Is Sir Tillman well? Has something happened to him?"

Geoffrey scowled as he sat down. "Sir Tillman is an ox and I would hardly make a visit to bring up the boy, now would I?"

Serena stifled the urge to smile. *Good. Let's make sure you're in no mood for declarations, shall we?* "It was an honest guess. You have never failed to bring him up previously, so why would I think this morning would be the exception? Where is he? Paying an early call on another elderly friend?"

"Damn it! You mean to make me jealous with this."

She blinked as if he'd accused her of flying. "Are you?"

Geoffrey smiled, a wicked knowing thing. "What an awkward gambit, Raven! Come, come. You already revealed your desires to me and I—"

"That is not my name." She leaned over abruptly and rang a small silver bell on the table. "This is most unseemly. If you'd let me know you were coming, propriety dictates that another party is present when a bachelor calls on an unmarried woman in her home."

Albert appeared instantly in the doorway. "Your Ladyship?"

Lord Trent's confusion was palpable. "Do you mean to have me thrown out, Lady Wellcott? Without hearing what I've come to say?"

"A note would have been a wiser means to convey your thoughts. I enjoy a man who is as eloquent on the page as he is in person." She could feel the heat on her cheeks, inspired by memories of Trent's letter to Phillip so many years before. God knew that no one could imprint parchment with the blackness of their soul more skilfully than the earl. Serena rose from her chair, preparing for his dismissal. "Your rival holds the advantage there."

Geoffrey mistook the pink in her cheeks for feminine pleasure. "You like notes, do you?" Lord Trent leaned back in his seat, his gaze narrowing. "What was in that message you received at the theatre? Was it from Adam? Or from another man? What rival thinks to insinuate himself between us? I will have all of it. You'll tell me. You know I will have every detail from your lips."

"Your Ladyship?" Albert asked again and Serena held up her hand to hold the footman in place.

"I understand it is raining this morning. I do hope you remembered an umbrella, Lord Trent. Thank you so much for calling." She leaned in to lower her voice as if she feared the footman would overhear. "You are rusty at this, Geoffrey. But here is a detail you can think on until I agree to see you next. *If* I had ambitions to marry, *why* would I invite you to ruin my reputation by making uninvited calls to destroy my social chances of achieving that goal? You make a woman ineligible before you're off the blocks."

Geoffrey's eyes widened and he unfolded from the chair. "I see. I see. How very wise and calculating of you, duchess. But let us disregard this small visit as one of a familial nature. Yes? After all, as far as the world is concerned, we are practically family, Lady Wellcott."

She raised her eyebrows in an arched look of surprise. "I see. And why would a man with familial connections be ranting about like a jealous bantam rooster in my sitting room over my private correspondence? Or is it that you wished to bark disapproval of his attentions? Are you now invoking a parental role, Lord Trent? How utterly confusing!"

"No! I'm—damn it! You are deliberately twisting my words!"

"Good day, Lord Trent." Serena raised her voice, radiating what authority she could muster but gifted her nemesis with a bone-melting smile to ensure he was as off-balance as a toddler. "I'm afraid I have a busy schedule today and must press on. So kind of you to call."

Albert took one step forward but it was enough.

"Yes, yes!" Trent sighed and raked his fingers through his hair. "I should have...brought the Tree."

"A tree?" Serena asked.

Lord Trent smiled, his humor fully restored. "Never you mind, Lady Wellcott. I will see you out and about, then, and I shall follow the steps of this dance. As you say, I am a bit rusty but not for long. You wish to savor the formalities? Very well. I can see how the illusions might be precious to someone in your situation."

"Someone in my situation?" she asked.

Geoffrey nodded merrily. "Come, come, Lady Wellcott. You can bustle about and make a show of it all you wish, but at the end of the day, you are alone. What allies would come to your defense if pushed?

You, Lady Wellcott, are one pointed finger away from ostracism but do not fear. I won't betray your secrets and I am happy to play along with whatever game you choose."

"How generous of you."

"I'll make the most of this, duchess. After all, I am yet a man to be reckoned with and I do enjoy *winning*." He touched his forehead in salute and then strode out with Albert respectfully but firmly behind him.

She watched his retreat with what she hoped was the right balance between defiance and a woman overwhelmed with longing and excitement at the prospect of an earl's courtship—just in case the monster turned around for one parting glance.

She held her pose until she heard the front door closed and latched behind him and abandoned the effort immediately. Serena sat down slowly as if fearful that she would shatter and closed her eyes.

*The illusions might be precious to someone in my situation, he says? Dear God. Please come quickly, father. It seems you are exactly what is needed to clarify my "situation".*

Pepper spoke softly from the parlor door. "That was a surprise."

Serena smiled, opening her eyes, came to her feet to leave the room. She refused to display even a hint of weakness, not after yesterday's fits. "A good lesson that I am not nearly as clever as I thought. But I doubt he'll call again without ample warning. The storm has passed."

"Has it? Well, I don't mind saying I'm relieved to hear it. I swear, Mr. Quinn was readying a full assault team below stairs to burst in to your defense."

"A comforting notion," Serena lifted the front edge of her skirts to climb the stairs. "I should get bathed and dressed for that luncheon with Mrs. Marsh. I will want the pearl combs so I hope they are back from the jewelers."

Pepper followed her. "They were delivered yesterday. Only…"

"Only…what, Prudence?" Serena pivoted on the landing to face her maid.

"I hadn't seen him before. I—I imagined him so much more..." Pepper sighed. "I nearly expected horns and cloven feet."

Serena smiled, her eyes watering at her friend's sweet nature. "What a lovely life it would be, Pepper. But if every wicked creature were forced to wear horns, how in the world will I wear my favorite pearl combs?"

# CHAPTER 18

That night, after a late solitary supper in her rooms, Serena reread the note she'd received from Phillip. It was a playful invitation for her to meet him that night but after her encounter with Trent she was in no mood for dalliance. Instead, she wrestled with the phantom of her appetite and the earl's vague threats while pushing her food from one side of the plate to the other.

*I will need to choose the venue and then push him past reason if—*

Serena was startled by the distant sound of a bell at the front door. She bolted to her feet, instincts jangling.

*Trent!*

*Scandal be damned, he has circled back after stewing all day.*

Her hands shook as she adjusted her hair combs, grateful that at least she hadn't yet undressed for bed and could face him quickly—but this time she would give Quinn the nod to arm the footmen and let the chips fall where they may.

There was a soft knock on the door and Albert stepped inside. "The Duke of Northland has arrived, your ladyship. Would you like—"

She pushed past him, running down the stairs to hurl herself into her father's arms who stood in the grand foyer with his arms outstretched and waiting. He enfolded her in his embrace, his hands stroking the silk of her hair, and a dozen endearments whispered into her ears.

Here and for her, the most reserved man in all of England, clung to her and allowed her to do the same. "You came."

He nodded, relinquishing her only to make a parental inspection of his child, his approval shining from his eyes. "I'd have been here sooner but muddy roads are no respecter of rank. I am unhappy to report that cursing is also not effective in increasing one's speed. I left a cloud of obscenities over Surrey that may wilt gardens and destroy crops."

Serena laughed. "I knew I longed to see you but—until this moment, I didn't realize how very much it meant."

"Come, then. Let's sit and talk for a while and see if we cannot settle my nerves."

"Yes, of course. Mr. Quinn, can you ask Mrs. Holly to bring up a supper tray for the duke and see that a draft of fresh lemonade is included. We'll be in the upstairs study." She took his arm and they climbed to the second floor together. "It is one of my favorite rooms and best suited to conversation."

"Then lead on." He shook his head. "How in the world did you know of my fondness for lemonade? After all, it is not the usual drink of choice for a man my age!"

"You are teasing me, Your Grace. What diabolical mastermind would I be if I did not retain a few resources within your household?"

"Who? Who are your spies?"

"A woman never divulges all of her secrets."

It was his turn to laugh. "Keep them, dearest. Oh, what a Walsingham you would have made!"

They settled by the fireplace in the sitting room, the dinner tray and drinks delivered before they'd shifted the cushions for comfort. Serena glowed with pride at the responsiveness of her staff, aware that Mr. Quinn was beside himself to have the Duke of Northland under the roof (even for a scandalously late call).

"Was there anything else, Your Grace?"

"No, thank you. I sent my luggage on and will be heading out later to my Town house, so please don't scramble the staff to prepare rooms or make a fuss. I will not impose on Lady Wellcott for long."

Quinn retreated with a bow and Serena sighed. "You are never an imposition, Your Grace."

"Says the gracious hostess," he countered. "But what an oaf I am! I meant to wish you a happy birthday as my first words and then the sight of you bolting down those stairs like a colt drove every civilized blessing from my head."

"Is it?" Serena asked. "I…missed it completely."

Northland shook his head. "You are twenty-five years of age today, my darling, and I—I could not have forgotten the day even if I tried." His eyes took on a sad and faraway look. "No, nor should I."

She reached out to touch his hand, a small gesture of comfort. She had learned from him that her mother died giving birth to her and the pain of it haunted him to this day. The Duke of Northland had never recovered and never married. She tipped her head to one side to study him quietly. He was not yet to his fiftieth year and a part of her wondered if fate might provide for his happiness.

He looked up, startled at his own lapse into silence. "I'm apparently more tired than I knew if I'm reduced to a maudlin fool in front of you."

"You are never foolish." Serena smiled. "Again, I am just glad you received my letter."

"I love all your letters. Even if they are generally sweetly fictitious," he sighed.

"What are you accusing me of, Your Grace?" she asked.

"Your heart betrays you, Lady Wellcott. I think you love your father too much to write of a single melancholy thought or incident. Your letters usually would have me believe that you are touched with nothing rougher than butterfly wings…"

"My last note must have been a jarring change then," she conceded. "Is that why you came so quickly?"

He nodded. "I would give you the moon if you dared look at it longingly in my presence, and you know it. And so you ask for nothing, wary of taking advantage of an old man's firm attachments, Lady

Wellcott. Imagine my surprise when you requested that I come to London to publicly appear next to you for some innocuous musical performance and party."

"Not a terrible surprise then?"

"It was a joy to feel needed—by my independent and beautiful child."

"It is a terrible tangle, isn't it?" she said softly. "I would do anything to make you happy but I cannot be less independent. I wish to keep you from worry and repay your kindness by shielding you from the madness of my world."

"Change nothing." He took a sip of his lemonade and grinned at her. "Just be yourself."

"I love you, Your Grace."

"Then call me father."

"Father." She smiled. The word pleased them both and she gently replaced one hand over his, wishing that there had been a simpler path to saying it to him. She had avoided the word in public for fear of humiliating him and then privately, stepped around it to cushion her heart from pain. "You deserve a better daughter."

He smiled, his eyes sad. "God help me, that you would love me despite our past, it still razes me to the bone."

"It would be unnatural to do any less, than care for you as I do."

"Then ask me to do more for you, Serena. A simple appearance and show of my acceptance of you is too paltry a thing."

She shook her head in wonder. "Did you have an example in mind?"

"I don't know." He sighed. "A new carriage? Another house? No, even as I hear myself talking, my soul is cringing. If I could I would wrench apart the heavens to give you whatever your heart desired."

She gripped his hand, her eyes filling with tears. "The only thing I desire is revenge against Geoffrey Parke and I must do it alone, Father. I would never inflict on your dear sweet person the agony of it. But I...have a plan in motion."

"Do you?"

"I only need you to remind Lord Trent that I have your full

support and devotion. I want him to respect me and temper his famil-iarity with my past with a renewed understanding of my father's interest in my happiness. He cannot see me as a vulnerable orphan somehow still in his debt."

"Does he?"

She shrugged. "I suspect he does and in his warped view, no show of wealth alters his opinion. But you... My instincts tell me that the sight of you will pull him up."

"That I can do easily. I will appease him and even make an insin-cere offer of friendship if that is what it takes. And," he leaned over to kiss her on the forehead. "I will do so wearing the new waistcoat you sent me for Christmas."

She smiled. "You do look more stately in that brocade."

"More like a duke? My wardrobe has improved in the last seven years to such an extent that my tailor confessed he was convinced that there was a new woman in my life."

"And there was," she said softly.

"My daughter." He looked down into her eyes, so very much like his own. "My life come back to me and my heart restored."

# CHAPTER 19

"Are you ready, dearest?" Northland asked as the carriage pulled to a stop in front of the grand entry to the Marquis of Sudbury's home. They were in a long line of carriages unloading their elegant passengers for the evening's concert and Serena stole a subtle look out the curtains to admire the pageantry.

"Soldiers' before the trumpet calls an advance would envy my readiness, Your Grace."

"I don't doubt it."

"And you? Are you sure that you are ready for this?" she asked in return. "They may snap at your heels for trotting your bas—"

"I hate that word, Serena." He cut her off. "I forbid you to use it again. As for me, I am made of sterner stuff. I don't care if dowagers start fainting and falling like autumn leaves in there. I want Trent to know what manner of father I am."

"Then let's show him."

At last it was their turn to alight and Serena let out a slow breath. She wasn't exaggerating. Tonight's challenge felt light enough. A runner had already confirmed that both Lord Trent and Sir Tillman would be in attendance. The Duke of Northland's presence would be enough to hold Geoffrey in check, the minor flurry of gossip caused by the Duke's public show of acceptance toward his unacknowledged offspring was a small price to pay. She would gain in social stature and power within minutes what it took others years to build.

Never before had she publicly taken her father's arm.

"Northland!" The Marquis of Sudbury greeted them inside the house. "I am honored beyond words to have you here."

"Julian, may I present the incomparable Lady Serena Wellcott?"

The marquis' expression was priceless as he took in the striking sight of his friend's pale grey eyes mirrored and framed with black lashes reworked in exquisite beauty as Serena offered him her gloved hand. "Yes...of course," he said softly.

"A pleasure to meet you again, your lordship."

Julian looked at the duke and then back at Serena. Side by side, there was no denying the connection. "Naturally, we've met before haven't we? I just cannot believe I—could have forgotten such a thing. Well, I have seats saved for you both next to my wife and I for the best experience."

It was also an open show of support and the Duke of Northland shook his friend's hand again. "Thank you, Julian."

The duke escorted her into the grand salon which had been converted into a small performance hall for the night. He made a point of greeting acquaintances, introducing her as he went and Serena nearly forgot her purpose as she basked in her father's smiles.

"Lady Wellcott? Is that you?"

Serena looked to see none other than Lady Hodge-Clarence approaching with a very cautious Mrs. Foxwood on her heels.

"It is. Good evening, ladies. Have you met the Duke of Northland? Your Grace, may I present Lady Hodge-Clarence and Mrs. Foxwood?"

"Charmed." Northland kept his hands behind his back.

"Do you enjoy classical music, Mrs. Foxwood?" Serena asked innocently.

Both women struggled to hide their amazement at the unmistakable revelations of Lady Wellcott's bloodlines but Mrs. Foxwood in particular looked unsteady. "I...cannot say."

"The evening's performance should help you to an answer, I would guess." The Duke of Northland's expression was that of a man less than impressed. "A risk if you discover that you hate it, Mrs. Foxwood, for you'll endure the hour either way."

"Temperance!" Lady Hodge-Clarence tried to intervene. "We adore music, Your Grace. Adore it!"

He nodded. "Good evening then. Come, Lady Wellcott."

"Yes, Your Grace. If you'll pardon us, ladies."

They retreated smoothly as the duke grumbled quietly, "I've tasted bitters that were less sour than that pair."

"They serve their purpose."

"If you say so." Northland deliberately placed his hand over hers as it rested in the crook of his arm. "Ah! Here comes the chance for me to fulfill *my* purpose."

Lord Trent hailed them from across the room and made his way toward his old friend, his expression neutral and wary. "I did not know that you were expected, Stephen. And Lady Wellcott... What a bracing surprise!"

"Is it?" Northland eyed Adam. "And who is this?"

"My nephew and sole heir, Sir Adam Tillman." Geoffrey extended his hand as if conjuring Adam from thin air. "Adam, this is the Duke of Northland, an old dear friend of mine."

"Tillman. Why does that name strike me as familiar?" Northland asked as they shook hands.

Adam shook his head. "I would be astonished, Your Grace, for I don't remember a previous meeting. Good evening, Lady Wellcott. You look lovely as always."

Serena smiled shyly and kept her eyes on Adam, deliberately ignoring Trent. "It is sweet of you to say."

"Didn't an Adam Tillman publish a paper at the Royal Science Academy? Something to do with Brunel's theories on drainage in tunnel construction?" the duke offered.

"A variation of them, yes." Adam smiled. "It was an obscure accomplishment but I'm flattered to have it recalled."

Lord Trent's smile dimmed but he pushed on. "I forgot your penchant for academic and useless trivia, Stephen."

"Did you?" The duke's expression darkened. "May I pull you aside for a word, Geoffrey? I'm sure Sudbury won't mind if we use his private study."

Lord Trent's mouth fell open, his eyes darting to his nephew and Serena who looked perfectly content at the arrangement. "I d-don't mind at all."

"Sir Tillman, if you would keep Lady Wellcott's company until my return, I would be grateful."

"Of course."

"I leave her to your care." The duke touched Adam's arm then led a contrite Lord Trent away.

Serena sighed as she watched them go, then turned back to Adam. "I have not seen you for several days. I'd begun to fear that you'd met with a terrible fate."

"I might say the same of you." Adam cleared his throat. "May I call on you, Lady Wellcott? I need to talk to you alone as soon as possible and frankly, this does not seem the place for the topic I have in mind."

"That sounds mysterious." She tipped her head to one side, assessing the intensity in his gaze. "Lady Lylesforth has already asked to come for tea tomorrow. Would you like to come afterward? Shall I ask her to stay?"

"At the risk of sounding like a madman, please don't. By all means, have your maid in the room or six footmen for propriety's sake, but I don't want to be the cause of gossip and I'm not sure a titled lady is the audience needed."

She nodded. "Very well. I will see you at six. My curiosity has over-ridden the usual objections to this unusual request, Sir Tillman."

The lights flickered to signal the need for all the guests to take their seats and Adam gallantly offered her his arm. "May I walk you in?"

"You are fearless, Sir Tillman." Serena took his arm, marveling at the simple twists of her evening.

"As are you, Lady Wellcott."

* * *

"TRENT." The marquis private study was as opulent a library as any Northland had seen but he paid it scant attention. Geoffrey was his sole focus and he wasted no time in getting to the distasteful business at hand. "How has it been so many years since you've crossed my path?"

"Your Grace," Geoffrey nodded, openly pleased. "Our Raven has—"

"Don't. I spent too much money and too much effort to clean the slate to have you so casually befouling things now." The duke's gaze was cold granite. "I do wish to say something to you, old friend."

"Of course."

"I blamed you for a long time, for my daughter's downfall. But I think wisdom has intervened. Who can stop the wind or command a river not to run? Youth makes us impulsive and she inherited my headstrong will. I don't think any guardian could have prevented that villainous Warrick from taking advantage."

The Earl of Trent nodded quickly. "If you only knew how I fought to keep the baron at arm's length and discourage the affair!"

"Serena has made it all clear."

"Has she?"

"She has a good view of things and an instinct for balance. As you know, I have a *great* interest in her happiness."

"Of course you do. You are not the kind of man to lose track of your treasures."

The duke held very still. "No. Especially the priceless and irre-placeable ones."

"Come, let's share a brandy and toast this reforged alliance." Trent led him over to the side table where crystal decanters gleamed in the firelight. "You do still enjoy a good glass, my friend?"

Northland nodded slowly. "On rarer occasions. I drank more than my share in my younger years as you well know."

Geoffrey laughed. "I admire a man with a good appetite, whatever his proclivities."

"Odd that I never could guess where your pleasures lay." North-land kept his hands behind his back. "It makes you harder to trust, sir."

"Truly? I suppose my greatest joys are found in..." Lord Trent tipped his head to one side as if waiting for a voice inside his head to whisper a good answer. "In a good game. I like to win, but even better, I like to make sure the rules are set so that my victory is assured."

"Your greatest pleasure is cheating?" the duke asked in astonishment.

"I don't see it in those terms!" Trent smiled. "Only weak men believe that they are at the mercy of the fates, Northland. I have never accepted that lie. And anyone who thinks to push me aside or underestimate me, there is no greater thrill than teaching them the error of their ways."

"A man would be a fool to underestimate you, Lord Trent."

"I think I will marry, Your Grace. A young woman who will give me an heir and it will be my nephew's turn to taste defeat at my hands. He thinks to climb over my carcass with the ease of a field laborer climbing a fence to take what he believes is his due. My sister has probably filled his head with tales of the wealth and charm of Oakwell Manor. Stupid woman!"

"A young woman…" The duke's gaze narrowed. "Pardon me, Geoffrey, but you look…the years have not necessarily been kind."

"What? I am—I am yet a man in his prime! My looking glass confirms it daily." Trent's smile was not as bright at the affront. "This from a man teetering into his dotage!"

Northland smiled slowly. "I have the vigor of a man half my age. You can ask my mistresses if you don't believe me."

"Mistresses? As in plural?" Geoffrey gave him an openly assessing look. "I would not have guessed it of you."

Northland said nothing.

"Come. You have just put our past aside to admit that I have been a friend to you and to your daughter all along. Tell me your secret if you have one to this unprecedented stamina! Man to man, do you owe me any less?" Trent pressed him quietly.

"Very well. I have discovered a special tonic and can tell you in confidence that as a result, I have fathered more children than I can keep track of in recent years. I am renewed, sir." The duke poured himself a brandy. "Forgive me. I spoke out of turn and forgot my natural reserve. You are too charming, old friend. I always did have a terrible habit of sharing too much with you."

"There is nothing terrible in that," Geoffrey said quickly. "Only terrible if you hint at this elixir and do not share the source with me!"

Northland shook his head. "It is for potency and sexual prowess and not a thing to be bandied about, Geoffrey. At five hundred pounds sterling a bottle, I am not sure you have the wallet for this treatment."

"I am not light in the purse. I can easily pay as much for such a thing if it means that I can satisfy a lusty young wife."

"A *lusty* young wife?" Northland asked. "Until tonight, you have said nothing of abandoning your bachelorhood. But if it truly is in the honorable pursuit of a wife and fulfilling your duties at last, then I shall send you a bottle at my own expense and wish you well. Consider it a token between us. Take a small dose each day, no more than a drop or two and soon the effects will be unmistakable. By the time you wed, you will be as randy as a sailor and guaranteed of an heir. But see that you don't share it with anyone else. I find I like my reputation as a recluse and have no wish to be petitioned endlessly by whoring fools and be known for such a thing!"

Trent shook his head. "You always worried too much about your reputation, old friend."

"You may be right, but you'll keep this secret all the same."

"All the same," Trent said as he lifted his own glass and the men toasted to their friendship.

Northland looked at him over the rim of his glass, pretending to drink. His weakness for alcohol was a demon he was not foolish enough to release again. He spit the alluring liquid back into his glass as smoothly as he could, tasting only sadness.

*He's right. I worried too much about my reputation. I turned my back on my darling girl, lost her to childbirth and then did little more than abandon our child for fear that others would judge me.*

*My Raven wishes me to befriend you for her schemes and so I have...*

*I only pray this wife you've selected gives you nothing but misery before you fall into your grave one day, Trent.*

# CHAPTER 20

*I*t was a stolen morning with Phillip before the next day's social calls commenced. They'd made love most of the morning and then dressed to share a brunch and lounge in her drawing room, pretending as if nothing beyond the walls existed to effect their lives. He read the paper while she sorted her correspondence and wrote in her journal.

The quiet held an allure all its own and Serena finally looked up to survey him, handsome and lean, his expression serious as he absorbed an editorial on land reforms.

"I must stop this," Serena said.

Phillip looked up. "What are we ceasing exactly?"

"This. It's dangerous, you know. If I had any common sense at my command I would truly exile you until after…it won't be much longer and I will be entirely free, Phillip. Why can I not be sensible when it comes to you?"

"You are the most sensible person I have ever met. Besides, I am already exiled, remember?"

"Hardly," she countered with a smile. "I would not describe you as a man banished to isolation these days."

"It's the turning point, isn't it?" He set his paper aside and crossed over to pull her into his arms.

She didn't answer him at first.

"No more secrets."

Serena yielded, looking up at him. "Yes. If I don't drop the reins, then I stand at the precipice."

"Tell me again who is jumping off cliffs and how deadly the fall."

"Do you trust me, Phillip?"

"I do absolutely." He reached out his hand to stroke her face. "Why? Why would you ask?"

"You may hear some gossip in connection with myself and...with Trent. I confess I've deliberately fueled most of it with an eye to— encouraging him."

"What am I going to hear?"

"Probably a rumor that I am madly in love and likely to be Lady Trent."

"Oh, God! To which generation have you supposedly lost your heart?"

She shrugged her shoulders very prettily. "The rumor is a bit non-specific."

"He could be strangling Adam as we speak, my darling." Phillip released her and crossed his arms, a dark cloud furrowing his brow.

"Not likely. I have given the man a great deal of hope and his pride and confidence will fill in every gap. No matter what anyone hints, he will make up his mind and paint himself the victor."

"Until he isn't?"

"Right up until the moment he isn't."

Phillip gently seized her upper arms, capturing her against his chest. "All right, Raven. Where? When? Tell me exactly."

"Pardon?" she asked, innocently feigning confusion.

"I've stood by long enough and while I won't directly interfere, if you think I'm not going to be present when this revelation hits Trent, you have lost your senses. I will be there to ensure that he doesn't snap your neck if nothing else. Do you hear me?"

"He won't snap my neck."

"That wasn't the main point I was trying to get you to acknowledge, Raven Wells."

"Fine. You will be there. You deserve to see it as much as anyone. But you will stay hidden from him until it's over, yes?"

"Yes."

"Very well. I will stay hidden. I will behave. I will do everything I can short of being invisible at this damn gathering but you have yet to answer the where and when."

"It will happen at Milbank's masked ball."

"How is it possible I didn't anticipate that it would be so soon? You said it was days but somehow I'd pushed it all out." His grip on her arms tightened. "And what if Sir Tillman hears this rumor and starts crowing a bit? What if he is offended to find out that it isn't true and makes a scene when you tell him otherwise? He could be the threat you haven't anticipated."

"Phillip, you're overthinking it. If Adam has heard it, he will disregard it or—"

"We are on a first name basis with Sir Tillman, are we?"

She said nothing for a few long seconds. "If you wish to accuse me of something, then do it. But we are not going to play this game, Warrick. Your jealousy of Sir Tillman is understood. You made no effort to hide your dislike of the man."

"I don't dislike him."

"Then stop growling! No matter what Sir Tillman believes, it won't amount to smoke after Milbank's, yes? My business with Trent will conclude and all will be revealed. I'm sure part of that chaos will involve an end to my friendship with Adam."

Phillip nodded slowly, his expression grim. "So long as you are not ended."

"Very well. Milbank's. But you're to attend unarmed, Phillip."

"No firearms." He held up one hand as if a man taking a solemn oath.

"No knives, poisons, or rabid dogs?"

Phillip struggled not to smile. "You are too clever for me. I will leave that twitchy terrier pup I was going to smuggle inside my evening coat in the carriage."

"That's my dearest love," she said then leaned forward to kiss him.

A knock at the door interrupted them and they both stepped back before Quinn made his appearance. "Lady Lylesforth to see you, madam."

"Thank you, Quinn. Give us just one moment and then by all means, escort her up."

Phillip sighed. "I'd complain more if I thought it would change anything. You're sure you've told me every—"

Serena punched him lightly on the arm. "I have told you everything I can! Now, Harriet is coming. I'd prefer not to have to explain you, Phillip."

"There's an idea!" He leaned over to tease kisses along the nape of her neck. "I could linger and play the fortune hunter, cause a scandal of my own, and trump the upcoming disaster in one fell swoop." His teeth gently nipped her skin as he spoke and she shivered with pleasure, her weight shifting against him to savor the contact. "What say you, Lady Wellcott? May I ruin you?"

"You are wicked, Sir Warrick," she sighed. "And I am already ruined."

"Then let me love you to restoration," he said.

"Go!" She pushed away from him. "Leave. It finishes in just three days and we will navigate together from there, I promise."

He kissed her hand and obeyed her one last time. "I will hold you to that promise, Raven."

She nodded and he left through the side door, just as he heard the other reopen as Quinn brought in her friend. He retreated as quietly through the house as he could, praying that this would be the last time he would feel like a thief sneaking away from her arms.


LADY LYLESFORTH SAT across from her, her usual dark plumage doing nothing to mute her beauty. Serena studied her friend and then sighed. "I wished to meet with you to reveal that this week at Milbank's costumed ball—it will be no ordinary social outing."

"No? In what way are we deviating from the usual course?"

"I want my chaperone to be particularly distracted and lax in her duties. You must dance and be quite occupied."

Harriet pressed her lips together, pursing them in disapproval. "Don't be ridiculous. I do not dance."

"You must." Serena set out the small tray with the sherry between them and then smiled at her friend's shock. "Now, now. One small sip with tea will not end you."

"What are you up to?"

"I want to have a drink with a dear friend to thank her for all her help and support. I want to make sure that you understand that my plans with Trent will probably come to their natural conclusion that night." Serena waited patiently as her announcement settled against Harriet's heart.

"Oh," Lady Lylesforth exclaimed softly, pressing her hand against her heart. "Will it be...dramatic?"

Serena nodded solemnly. "I certainly hope so."

"Is there anything else?"

Serena took a few minutes to give her the details of her role and a short list of the other Black Rose members she would need to educate during her social turns through the rooms. "If it goes the direction I desire, a chorus of opinion will seal his fate."

"I will see to it. But I am not going to pledge to dance."

"As you wish. I want to try to keep you clear of the blast."

"Is there to be an *explosion*?"

"Not literally," Serena said as she poured them both small glasses of sherry. "Though Lord Trent may have a different impression."

"I feel only a little better knowing that there will be other allies for you in that room. I would feel a great deal better if I were more confident of you calling on them for aid when the time comes."

"You cannot have everything you want, Harriet."

"A lesson I am well versed in, Serena." Harriet's eyes flashed with rare mischief. "But I can come close."

"How are your little beauties?"

"I love their dark sweet faces and darling noises. I cannot imagine my days without my pugs, Lady Wellcott. But then, I have you to thank for—"

Serena reached over to gently squeeze her hand. "Your happiness is thanks enough. One day, when it is all said and done, I shall think of you and the women of the Rose and it will be more than enough to see me through."

"Nonsense. There are debts that can never be repaid." Harriet's smile faded. "I don't care what you claim about shedding our woes. When I think of the burdens you carry for all of us, it makes me shudder."

Serena released her hold and sat up, stiffening her back with a sigh. "If I truly carried your burden, then you would be wearing pink. Don't think I don't know what goes on in that head of yours! You divert yourself with rules and punish yourself with widow's weeds for a man you loathed because you don't feel as guilty as you think you should."

Harriet blinked back tears. "I did loathe him. I wish I could stop hating him."

"You need to fall in love, Harriet." Serena held up a hand to stifle the inevitable protest Harriet was about to blurt out. "You pretend to hate all men but that hardly seems useful. You need to give in to a passionate love. Not a polite, cautious thing, not a social exercise in a proper courtship or an acceptable match. You need to lose yourself in a man's arms and discover the magic of a ridiculously heated tumble."

"I—I most decidedly do *not*!"

"Life is not life if you do not break the rules, my friend."

"That is precisely the sort of thing people say who write their own rules and seek to convince others to do the same." Harriet stood, shifting her bustled skirt to prepare to leave. "A man is the last thing I need, Lady Wellcott, of that you can rest assured."

Serena smiled, standing as well. "As you say."

"I will see you at the ball."

"Yes, my dearest Dragon. I will be there, no fear."

WHEN THE DOOR bell rang at six, Quinn brought Adam into the first floor drawing room as directed and Serena signaled for the door to remain slightly open as a scant nod to the requirements of propriety.

"Would you care to sit down, Sir Tillman?" She sat next to him on the settee, a respectable distance but in a far more intimate arrangement than she had ever allowed Trent. "I'll admit I've been fighting feminine curiosity ever since you asked for this interview. I'd accuse you of using a ploy or snare but the purpose of that deception was even harder to guess at…"

"I'm sorry. It was not my intention to cause you any anxiety." He let out a long slow breath. "I wanted to talk to you about Lord Trent."

"Lord Trent?"

"His interest in you grows more tenacious by the day. I thought to dissuade him from bothering you but instead, I fear I've spurred him on." Adam shifted on the cushions. "It's as if any mention of your name is taken as an open challenge of his powers."

"His interest?" She held very still. "What possible interest could he have in me? Perhaps you have misunderstood?"

Adam shook his head firmly. "No. There is no mistaking his intentions. He has laid plans to marry you."

"He never has!" Serena pressed a hand to her heart. "That's preposterous!"

"He's set on it, Lady Wellcott."

"Why have you taken it on yourself to…tell me of this?"

Adam's eyes darkened. "Honor would dictate that I say nothing against him but I'll be damned if I'm going to sit politely quiet while events unfold. Uncle Geoffrey is not entirely sane. Weeks in his company and I have no doubt when it comes to his capacity for erratic behavior. This is no playful flirtation, Lady Wellcott. There is something wrong, some sharp fault in his character that…" Adam leaned forward, the sincere concern in his face beyond question. "I don't know where this will go but I don't want to see you harmed."

Serena's heartbeat accelerated and she prayed that her skill for theatrics could sustain her. "You are very kind to think of protecting me but—I hardly think Lord Trent is capable of more than a fit over a lost card game. Sir Tillman, perhaps he is threatened by your youth and vitality and it affects his mood? You are seeing the uglier side of his temperament, I fear, but the face that I have seen is quite familiar." She smiled, a woman calm and in control. "The man I have encountered clings to bachelorhood like a drowning man to a raft. He derides any hint to the contrary, Sir Tillman."

Adam wasn't having it. "No. Hear me. There is no logic to any of this. Why would he play the disinterested fool to you and then screech about his own library about how I am the poacher who trespasses on his hunt?" He briefly pressed his hand to his forehead, steeling himself for speech. "I do not mean to shock or offend you, Lady Wellcott. It is a grim and messy business."

"It is." She nodded slowly. "Not the language I would expect to hear connected to a courtship, sir."

"No. On that, we agree."

Serena sighed. "He did call without warning the other morning. It was a strange visit but I—"

"What morning? When did he make this call?" Adam asked.

"Saturday."

"Damn it!" Adam cursed then she read the instant regret at the slip on his face. It was endearing and made her stomach hurt. "My sincere apologies, Lady Wellcott. I didn't realize he'd gone out without me."

*He's a good man. He's being so careful with me, so protective and watchful. But he cannot be allowed to stop Trent. I have to reassure him enough to stand aside...and to keep him from Geoffrey's reach.*

"If you have appointed yourself as his chaperone, you may be in for a terrible chase," Serena said. "He'll treat it like a game of hide-and-seek simply to torment you, Sir Tillman."

"What made the earl's visit strange, Lady Wellcott?"

"I am embarrassed to say it but he made an unsolicited offer of a loan. Apparently, the earl is convinced that I am penniless and intent on stealing your inheritance." Serena smoothed out her skirts, blushing. "So you see, I was once again to be schooled in my ineligibility though this time in the guise of an offer of charity. Hardly a romantic pursuit."

"That makes no sense."

"No. But for the sake of clarity, let me say once and for all, I have a substantial income, Sir Tillman. I own several properties, employ nearly a hundred servants and…well, without providing a financial accounting of myself, I am decidedly not a pauper. I told your uncle the same."

"What is he up to?"

"Keeping me out of your path, I suspect. I'm sure he thinks a woman is easier to steer than a grown man who knows his own mind." She studied Adam's face. "He can speak without a nod to civility to me without fear, but to you…he should mind his step."

Adam's smile held no warmth. "He has no right to be unkind to you. But may I ask you something terribly frank?"

"Of course. I think we've gone too far in this conversation to turn back now, Sir Tillman."

"Why don't you hate my uncle?"

"Pardon?"

"As a man who was once your guardian, his behavior is stinging to behold. He's like a charming rabid dog and I can't help but wonder how you could not feel that sting and not—hate him just little bit for it?"

"You don't think I hate him a little bit?"

"You are always smiles and lightness in his presence. It's disconcerting."

Serena held her breath, refusing to drop her gaze. "It's a sign of my cowardice, Sir Tillman. I know how cruel he can be. I know it firsthand. If I am light and smiles, it's because I fear that moment when his humor fails and he forgets to try. I am entirely human. I hate him more than a little bit, sir. But that is my burden to carry and I see no advantage to letting him or anyone else know how much."

"I shouldn't have pressed you on this. I'm sorry. It is wrong but you wouldn't believe the flood of relief I'm experiencing to hear it from your lips. At least I know you will stay safely out of his clutches—and we'll just let him rail all he wants."

"Please don't repeat what I've said. I shared it as a confidence because of our friendship."

"Your secrets are safe with me and I find that I am coming to think of you as one of my best friends in this world, Lady Wellcott." He caught her hand. "I want nothing more than to keep you safe."

Serena's heart hammered against her ribs. It was ridiculous. She should be melting against him and encouraging all of it as part of the game, but there was something so vulnerable in his eyes and she was alarmed at the heat that surged through her frame at it.

"As your friend, I should remind you that you are...I am not...I think you should hold hands with a more suitable young lady...or..."

Adam kissed her, a tender thing that had more of an inquiry in it than a commanding statement. For Serena, it was strange and surreal. She was still aching from an afternoon spent making love to Phillip, her body still sore from the exercise but Adam's touch evoked desire all the same. Her desire was raw and visceral, without any emotional edge. There was no history here. No dark past. No baggage or guilt.

She pushed him away.

"Forgive me."

"There is nothing to forgive. The fault is mine. Entirely mine." Serena turned and ran from the room, from Adam's arms and the betrayal of her senses. She bolted up the stairs of her house to the sanctuary of her bedroom in a race to outpace her tears and the tangle of her emotions.

He was innocent.

*But I am not! I am most decidedly not.*

\* \* \*

"What's happened? You look ill." Pepper set aside the dressing gown she was carrying, hurrying forward to see to her mistress. "What's wrong?"

"Why did I ever promise to keep no secrets from Phillip Warrick?"

Serena pressed her fingers against her cheeks. "I cannot...share my feelings with Phillip, not without risking a terrible misunderstanding. I think the days of revealing my thoughts to the man have been suspended for a time."

"Is it Sir Tillman?"

Serena nodded miserably. "How can I thoughtlessly crush a dozen men and laugh, but now—it's all changed. I hate it. I hate every lie I am forced to tell Adam and every lie I am forced to tell Phillip. And I cannot help but wonder..."

"Say it."

"That if my life had been different, if I were different, if—Adam Tillman is precisely the sort of man I would have set my cap for if we'd met my first London Season and if Phillip Warrick had never come to Oakwell Manor."

"Except you don't have a cap. It's firmly in Sir Warrick's possession. That's a lifelong love, isn't it? Like they write about in those novels you roll your eyes when you catch me reading, and you know it."

"I know it. I love Phillip so much that it robs me of breath."

"Well, that doesn't sound pleasing."

"It's a tangle. Loving Phillip has made me kinder...softer. So now I feel guilty about Adam! It's all Phillip's fault!"

"Oh, that's stuff and nonsense!"

"You're right. It's no one's fault but mine. I knew I liked Adam and admired him altogether. I should never have allowed him to kiss me."

"What?! He kissed you! There was kissing? Was it lovely?" Pepper squeaked.

"Pepper!"

"Well? A maid has a right to ask these things!" Pepper protested without a smidge of apology in her sparkling eyes. "I'd warrant it was a good and proper kiss by the way you're hissing and spitting over there."

Serena gave her friend a warning look. "Trent is destroyed, Adam goes on to marry an heiress spun from sugar, Phillip loves me and I reclaim my sanity. That is the *only* outcome I will accept."

# CHAPTER 21

*P*hillip placed his calling card on the silver tray the butler extended and then waited in silence as the man retreated to make his presence known. He did not pace or inspect the contents of the room, refusing to give in to nerves. The likeliest event would be a refusal to admit him and Phillip steeled himself for the possibility. He would leave without argument.

*I will have to reconsider how many days in a row I'll make the attempt before he calls the authorities or has me shot for—*

"He will see you, Sir Warrick. If you will follow me." The butler's announcement redirected his thoughts and Phillip trailed after the man out of the sitting room, through the grand entry and up the wide marble staircase. It was a palatial home, compensating for warmth with a soul-crushing show of wealth.

Phillip anticipated being shown into a library or study but was thrown off when the room he was led into was quite obviously a great bedroom and private sitting room. A dark carved four poster bed the size of a carriage dominated one end of the room, burgundy silk velvet drapery pooling onto the floor, ornate enough to offer an emperor and Phillip couldn't help but stare at the thing.

"Ridiculous, isn't it?"

Phillip shifted to spot the Duke of Northland sitting in his morning coat at a desk near the fireplace at the room's opposite end. "I can't imagine sleeping there. I think I'd be too distracted by the...craftsmanship."

The duke didn't reply, merely gesturing for Phillip to approach.

Phillip moved to stand before him. "I am grateful that you would see me, Your Grace."

"Warrick. Phillip Warrick." Northland made an open study of him from head to toe. "We meet at last."

"Yes." A thousand speeches abandoned him. A thousand reasons for taking this risk and pushing into the man's presence fled his mind's hold. A thousand bids for pardon vanished. *Damn it.*

The duke stood. "There was a time, Sir Warrick, when I did not think to hate another human being more than I hated you."

"Yes," Phillip managed.

"She came to me so...broken. She'd walked the heels off of her shoes and the weather had so destroyed her clothes, that a group of village boys mistook her for a beggar. Those little animals pelted her with rocks and mud, Phillip. Can you imagine it? *My* child reduced to an object of scorn and ridicule? *My* blood begging for a place in my kitchens? The creature who is the very image of her beautiful dead mother on her knees asking me softly if she could scrub my pots and pans in return for crusts of bread?"

Phillip shook his head, unable to speak past the lump in his throat.

"Crusts of bread, Warrick." The duke walked toward one of the massive windows that looked out onto regal gardens and stared down. "I said I did not think to hate another human being more than you. Can you guess who I hate more, Sir Warrick?"

"Trent."

The duke shook his head. "I have an ocean of loathing for that man but he is not the soul I have in mind."

"I cannot imagine it. I don't think anyone dead or living could edge out my villainy in your eyes."

Northland turned back to face him. "You are wrong. You see, there is one more man to be blamed for her downfall and he is the blackest villain of all. He is me."

"No," Phillip protested in shock. "That seems unlikely!"

"I was a weak drunkard and so full of vanity and pride, it sickens me to think of the way I swaggered through my youth, Warrick. I seduced a virtuous and beautiful creature and told myself that my desire and need were all the justification required. Then I fell in love with her." Northland sighed. "When she came to me in tears to tell me that there was to be a child, my father threatened to disown me. He threatened scandal, poverty and even exile if I married her—and I nearly held firm and defied him. *Nearly.*"

Northland began to pace in front of the fireplace, astonishing Phillip with the familiarity of a habit he'd seen Raven enact dozens of times.

"For my father demonstrated what ruthlessness really looked like. He hauled me down into the servant's hall and lined up no less than six pretty maids I'd tumbled in the previous year. He mocked my protests that I had reformed, he dared me to claim that I hadn't already fathered a bastard to two, he likened my darling to a common servant, and cruelest of all, told me he would be sure to introduce my future duchess to every slice of quim I'd plundered and make sure there was no question in her mind of what a worthless whoring rake she'd spread her legs for."

"My God."

"He made promises to provide for Arabelle and I...I was so humili-ated and weak, I allowed it. I fled to London and drank myself into a stupor so foul and all-encompassing that by the time I lifted my head from a puddle of my own vomit, Arabelle was dead. My father had lied, providing nothing for her support. The birth of our daughter proved too much for her and I learned later from the midwife that she had died of a broken heart."

"You couldn't have known what was to happen."

"I arranged for Raven's care without ever seeing her. The midwife knew of a childless vicar and his wife who had suffered their own losses. I instructed her to make the arrangements and then I never looked in that direction again. I returned to my drink and my grief, I nursed my hatred and inherited my title. I was twenty-two years old."

*Shit.*

"By the time I heard of her orphaned status years later, I was barely fit. Drink had made me ill and Trent—Trent appeared like a savior offering to amend the situation and give Raven the care that she deserved. The rest, I believe you know the rest." Northland stopped pacing. "I recognize villainy when I see it because I am familiar with a looking glass, Warrick."

Phillip shook his head. "No. These are tragedies, not a testament to who you are. I refuse to paint you black and allow that to stand."

Northland smiled. "You defend me? I thought you had come to offer your own defense."

"What defense can I lay down? That I was also young when I earned Trent's displeasure? That I blindly followed my passions to a love I cannot relinquish? That I hurt her in a fit of rage that I will regret until the day I die? What help to tell you that I doubled back for her, that when I couldn't find her I lamed a horse racing to Oakwell Manor only to get another dose of Trent's vile poison? Six months of searching the same roads over and over because I needed to know what had happened but all the while, cowering in the dark begging God not to allow me to know the worst?" Phillip pressed his fingers to his temples to tame the spikes of pain there. "That the blackest moment came when I stopped looking? Is ignorance a defense if I acknowledge that I was terrified of being robbed of her memory so I tried hating her instead?"

"And now?"

"I love her. I never stopped loving her. She and I have reached a truce and I have vowed to never leave her again. I will spend the rest of my life striving to deserve her and doing whatever I can to make her happy."

"Marriage?"

"If she desires it. So far, she has refused to entertain it. Your daughter is a very independent creature and also somewhat...unconventional."

"Yes." Pride shone from Northland's eyes. "Yes she is."

"She is my life."

The duke's gaze narrowed. "Why are you here, Warrick?"

"I'm here because I don't know you. Because I think her business with Trent is about to come to a finish and in the crush of my worries for our future, I realized that I could not leave this alone. I will be a part of her life, Your Grace. If you hate me for what I've done, if you harbor resentment or a need for vengeance, then I wanted to make sure that I'd faced you openly. I want my debts paid so that there are no more phantoms haunting my steps. I've wasted too much time looking back over my shoulder. It ends today."

"You don't know me. What will you do if I start yelling for pistols at dawn?"

Phillip blinked. "I honestly hadn't gotten that far. I suppose I'd make the suggestion that your daughter won't forgive you for shooting me in an illegal duel and recommend making it look like an accident instead? You are a wealthy enough man to hire an assassin and prevent her from making the connection."

"True enough." Northland smiled grimly. "An accident, eh? Throwing yourself on my mercy. A huge risk considering that you really do not know me at all."

"Apparently a larger one than I'd anticipated." Phillip held his ground and waited.

Northland's expression changed, his smile betraying a flash of mischief in smoke-grey eyes. "My God, I like you! Sit down, Warrick. Have a lemonade with me and let's see if we cannot arrange for your survival."

The duke began to laugh as he rang for refreshments and Phillip found himself doing the same.

# CHAPTER 22

Geoffrey climbed down from his carriage, waving away the helping hand of the liveried footman. He rewarded the man with an icy look of reproof. He was not some dottering old man to require help down a step, for God's sake!

Trent's ill humor slid away as he acknowledged that he felt more like a boy escaping school. Adam had been particularly sticky the last few days, but he was not infallible. Geoffrey had diverted him for the afternoon with a manufactured, forged note from the Reform Club claiming that one of their most revered members wished to see him regarding an engineering project of vast urgent importance to Her Majesty.

*Stupid Trent! By the time he realizes it's a ruse, I'll be home with my feet up after a delightful day spent in the company of the delicious Lady Serena Wellcott—and several steps closer to putting a collar on my tigress.*

He had the vigor of a man of five and twenty these days and the notion that winning Serena also means snatching her out from under his sniveling nephew's nose makes the promise of victory ever sweeter.

A tantalizing bit of gossip had reached him just that morning and if the earl knew anything, he knew that a wise man struck while the iron was hot.

*Lady Wellcott is in the throes of some secret love, is she? Well, let us see if we cannot relieve her misery. Adam is an idiot but he is right about one thing. A woman like Raven needs a strong confident hand even if she is too proud to admit it.*

It was a small garden party, his least favorite kind of social gathering but he'd have sought an invitation to paper boat races if it afforded him an opportunity to publicly demonstrate his indifference to the lady. His plan was simple. He would torment her with his presence, following every little rule just beyond her reach, to drive her wild with wanting and force her to admit regret for her insistence on the formalities.

*I will reward my duchess with the mantle of respectability that comes with marriage and teach her what true carnal pleasures can provide to a hedonistic amoral little vixen.*

He walked through the house, ignoring the smaller gatherings of guests lingering inside for conversation and refreshments and made his way to the walled gardens. The weather was momentarily fair but dark clouds gathered in the east and Geoffrey marveled at people's talent for optimistically ignoring the looming signs of a typical summer rain. A good size lawn surrounded by low hedges and concentric walkways provided ample room and Geoffrey frowned as he realized that hoops had been set up across the grass with several people selecting mallets to begin a game of croquet.

*God, I hate croquet!*

The sound of feminine laughter arrested his attention and he spotted Serena amidst the players.

*God, I love croquet!*

He hurried over just as it appeared that they were dividing up into teams.

"Lady Wellcott, that means you have—"

"I should love the chance to partner with you, Lady Wellcott," Geoffrey said. "What say you?"

"Oh." Her surprise at his quick arrival warmed his blood. "A generous offer, your lordship, but we are playing as singles. Would you like to take the blue?"

He would rather have used the guise of partnering and mentoring her play to touch her publicly, but Geoffrey decided that he would make the most of the day. "The blue it is!"

Play commenced and Geoffrey made sure that he mirrored her moves as a subtle excuse to converse while they awaited their turns.

"Did you enjoy the music the other night, Lady Wellcott? It was... such a lovely surprise to see the Duke of Northland, was it not?" he asked sweetly.

*You sent for your father because you wished to give me the chance to ask for his blessing, didn't you, Raven? What a twist to find you old-fashioned when it comes to these matters!*

"It was a delightful performance," she conceded. "But after hearing your opinion on the theatre, I am wary of asking what you thought of it."

"How clever of you! A bunch of warbling violins and noise with a smattering of Italian thrown in, it's a wonder anyone wastes a moment." He bent over to make a brutal strike that sent her ball hurtling off the course. "I can think of better ways to spend an evening, can't you, Lady Wellcott?"

*There! There's indifference! I am not some fawning adolescent, am I? I am a man you will strive to please, Raven. Your every joy will be measured out by my generosity or not at all.*

She walked after her ball without complaint, smiling as the other players lamented her bad luck. Geoffrey frowned at the lack of a feminine pout or tempestuous stamp of a foot but play resumed.

Indifference was more challenging to manufacture than he'd anticipated as she coolly minded the strategy of hoops, her strikes keeping her just beyond his reach. She laughed and jested with several of the other ladies, cheering politely when they scored as if she cared nothing for her own points.

Geoffrey hated losing. It was a strange battle between his frustration at uncooperative croquet balls and his sexual frustration at a woman who floated in his peripheral vision.

*Humiliating! I should know better. How in the world does any man think to appear his best hunched over a stupid stick batting about colored balls? It's a woman's game, this!*

The sky had darkened gradually but when the heavens opened up into a cold downpour, Geoffrey nearly laughed at the blessings of Providence. Guests merrily scrambled for the cover of the house, ladies squealing in mild protest as their cloth parasols proved less than adequate protection from an English monsoon. He bolted toward Raven, thinking to offer her the haven" of his jacket over their heads but she thwarted him by opening her own parasol.

"Here. Let me walk you in, Lady Wellcott." He held out his arm but she kept both hands on the parasol handle.

"If you insist." She began to walk briskly toward the house and he jogged next to her, increasingly irritated by the fear that he looked like a puppy on her heels.

"Wait!"

She turned in surprise, thunder underlining the strangeness of his request. "I have no wish to drown, Lord Trent, nor to catch a chill. Come, we are nearly the last to get inside as it is."

He caught her by the waist before she reached the steps, aware that the angle of the verandah and stairs put them in a small pocket of invisibility from anyone looking out from the windows. Even the din of the storm gave them another layer of privacy and he reveled in it. "You used to love the rain. Remember? You would dance practically naked in the gardens until that nanny made such a fuss that we had to forbid it."

"I was a child then." She pushed against his chest and regained her freedom. "How dare you take liberties with my person! You'll keep your hands to yourself, your lordship."

"We are not meant for cautious rituals and restraint, my dear." Geoffrey watched the pink rise up in her cheeks and he knew he had her. "There is something feral in your nature, Lady Wellcott. I was the first to recognize it and I cannot help but think there is a lovely bit of irony within reach if I were ultimately the man to help you explore and expand that gift."

He reached for her again, intending to kiss her, but this time she eluded him, stepping away from the steps.

"Get back here! They'll see you!" He held out his hand, willing her to take it.

"Lord Trent. What do you know of me? I mean—of my nature?"

"You are a passionate creature. You always have been. Now, come kiss me, woman."

She shook her head. "You mistake me for a young girl who can be fooled by private seductions and secret declarations. I find I have a strong aversion to clandestine love affairs, Lord Trent. But I will not be made a whore for the world to see."

"I would never treat you that way. I mean to court you as slowly and cautiously as a woman has ever been courted, but you are driving me mad!" Geoffrey shifted on the steps. "One kiss."

"I cannot. You are right, Lord Trent. I am a passionate creature. I am—ruled by my passions. As a result, I do not dabble. I do not...play. Toy with someone else. You crafted me, Geoffrey. You made me what I am. My desires do not come in half measures or small doses. My reputation for abstinence is not borne from a lack of desire, but the opposite." She sighed. "We have always spoken plainly, you and I. So I will tell you that I am not willing to be fucked senseless within twenty yards of my charitable committee and several members of the House of Lords."

His eyes widened at her raw language, his posture betraying his immediate arousal as he shifted to try to hide it from her and he suspected she already knew he was her willing slave. "I wasn't going to...go so far."

"No?" She smiled, a wicked wanton smile that promised him the world. "As I said. I do not dabble. Do not insult me again by insinuating that I am willing to settle for less than *everything* you have to offer." She tipped her parasol back to allow the rain to anoint her hair and face, a pagan goddess evoking the worship of fire. "I require more than passion, Lord Trent."

*Everything I have to offer...yes!*

Before he could give his willingness a voice, she went on.

"Tomorrow night. I will be at Milbank's masked ball. Decide, Geoffrey, once and for all. Either you will step forward and *publicly* declare yourself at the height of the evening or you will never speak to me again. No half measures."

"No half measures," he echoed and she brushed past him up the stairs and disappeared into the house, leaving him to take a moment in the cold rain to try to gather his thoughts and cool his blood.

"To hell with half measures!" he said again, and then laughed. Milbank's was the perfect setting for his proposal of marriage, for Adam to have his public comeuppance and defeat and it was even the perfect place for a man to pull his warm and willing fiancé into an alcove to be fucked senseless into submission.

*Tomorrow night will be a night to remember for years to come!*

\* \* \*

SERENA BARELY MADE it home before the shock wore off.

Quinn took her coat, his expression one of alarm. "Your ladyship, you are soaked to the bone!"

"Lady Mortimer's lawn party may have not been the best choice for an afternoon's entertainment." She peeled off her wet gloves and shivered. "Can you alert Pepper that I'll need a hot bath as quickly as it can be arranged?"

"Of course."

Serna lifted the sodden weight of her skirts and climbed the stairs, ridiculously exhausted from the day. From an objective point of view, it had been a successful outing. She'd issued a direct challenge to Trent for Milbank's with no witnesses to any of it. If he'd skipped the garden party, she would have been forced to put pen to paper to issue her ultimatum. She was always reluctant to create tangible evidence of their connection.

Luckily, it hadn't come that.

But if she had any small doubts remaining about Trent's desires, they were gone.

She shivered again. *He is not my father—nor really an uncle but...oh, God, I nearly vomited on his shirt front.*

It was a visceral response she needed to get under control before the ball tomorrow night.

She achieved her bedroom and Pepper was just behind her. "You're as pale as a ghost!" Pepper moved quickly to help her undress. "And as cold as one, I'd warrant!"

Serena was about to toss out a clever retort but her teeth were chattering too much. Instead she pressed her lips together.

"That's bath's pulling together in the dressing room, and I'll make sure Mrs. Holly makes a nice nourishing broth part of the menu with dinner. Pneumonia is not what I'd have slated for your calendar this week, your ladyship."

"I'm not sick. At least, nothing that won't be cured by tomorrow night." Serena let out a long, slow breath to steady her nerves. "I hate Geoffrey Parke."

"I know it, your ladyship." Pepper pulled her dress free and the quickly helped her step out of her petticoats. "Maybe that devil will be the one to catch pneumonia and spare you all this effort."

"Ever the optimist!" Serena smiled. "But no. I will be extremely put out. If that man takes to his bed with a fever and dies, I'll be forced to find a witch doctor, resurrect him and throttle him all over again."

"I do love it when you talk like that, your ladyship! I know I shouldn't but it's such a dark little thrill, isn't it?" Pepper helped her into a warm robe and slippers. "I'll check on the bath and get a soothing draught from downstairs. You just rest here for a bit and—"

"Pepper. You are not to send for Phillip."

"Oh! I wasn't...I would never..."

Serena put her hands on her hips. "Never?"

"How did you know!?"

Serena smiled. Not for all the gold sovereigns in the British Empire would she admit that she hadn't been completely sure until Pepper's blurted question. "Sir Warrick's timing has been impeccable lately, hasn't it? Arriving just when I needed him most or sending a note after Trent called without warning."

Pepper's chin lifted a fraction of an inch, her tiny soul bracing for the firing squad. "I only wished you to be happy. No man's an island and all that!"

"Prudence. Do I look angry?"

Pepper's defensive posture faltered. "N-no, which is frightening me all the more, I'll have you know!"

Serena smiled and pulled her into her arms for an embrace. "Thank you, Prudence. I could not ask for more in a friend."

"Nor I."

Serena freed her hold, both of them blushing a little at the awkward display. "Now hear me. I shall be the one to send for Phillip when the time warrants it. No more schemes of your own, Pepper. Agreed?"

Pepper nodded solemnly. "Yes, your ladyship."

"Very well. See to that bath, omit the draught and let Quinn know that I am absolutely in for the night. I'll see no one until Milbank's."

"Sir Warrick may wish to—"

"I'll send him word. Pepper. No one until Milbank's."

Pepper nodded and left through the door into the dressing room.

She walked to the window and pulled the curtains to look out at the rain. It had never relented and she sighed at the memories it evoked. Invoked on Trent's lips, he'd defiled her ancient joy but Raven forced herself to recall it now, to reclaim the element for herself.

*I was the daughter of the King of Clouds. The rain was the way he sang to me and I told myself that every cold drop was a kiss on my skin.*

"I'm a pagan wild thing, after all," she whispered and the warmth of her breath fogged the glass. "But I've got the Devil in hand so let's see where I can lead him."

# CHAPTER 23

*W*ith the solemnity of a knight emerging from a vigil, Serena dressed for the masked ball. The gown that Madame Montellier had crafted was nothing shy of a work of art. Silver lace woven in metallic threads cascaded in echoes of a bridal gown but she looked like a woman marrying the man in the moon. She was a creature of ice and silvery fire. The dress's bustle was encrusted with hundreds of clear glass crystal beads to capture the light and refract like diamonds.

The dress for this ball was one she'd chosen with deliberate care. The layers of shimmering lace in the bustle and along the décolletage made it a more youthful style than her usual cut silks and clean lines. Tonight, she purposefully evoked her youth, highlighting it and making a tasteful echo of the debutante she once might have been.

"It's a wintry waterfall, isn't it?" Pepper sighed as she rearranged the folds of the short train. "Every man in that room is going to fall under your spell tonight, your ladyship."

"Do you have the tiara ready?"

Pepper nodded and pulled it out. The current fashion leaned toward heavier jewels but Serena had selected a delicate headpiece that appeared to be carved from ice, as if the tiny diamonds would

melt if a human hand touched them. Nested atop a careful arrangement of plaited braids, one long ornate braid encircled with a silver
ribbon trailed down her back.

"You'll want your diamond choker," Pepper asserted.

Serena shook her head. "No. I'll wear the long silver chain and
nothing else."

"Not even the earrings?"

Serena smiled. "Not even the earrings." She wanted nothing to
detract from the bare lines of her shoulders and the firm white
column of her throat.

Pepper lifted the long silver chain over her head, the filament so
fine it was like a spider web that the gold ring strung on it almost
appeared to float magically through the air. It was a simple ring inlaid
with pale blue topaz and diamonds. It disappeared in between her
breasts and Serena smiled. That little ring was the one that Phillip had
given her to celebrate their wedding and now against her heart, it was
a talisman to signify her love for the man and the strength of the bond
between them.

The ritual of dressing calmed her but Serena could not deny her
nerves. Pepper was as anxious as she was, her hands trembling as she
knelt to help Serena step into her silver slippers. "Mistress. No matter
what happens, I hope you'll…"

"Pepper."

"I just want you to be happy."

Serena sighed. "I will be."

Pepper stood. "You think he'll cry like a toddler?"

She did her best to smile. "My life would feel complete if he did."

"Well, best get on your way then." Pepper held very still.
"Good luck."

"Thank you, Pepper."

She started to leave but Pepper called out, "The mask! Here! We
nearly forgot it!"

Serena took the matching scrap of silver lace and walked out
without looking back. She wasn't comfortable with maudlin scenes

and any more delays tempted her to say too much. She did not trust her voice to good-byes.

Mr. Quinn waited for her downstairs. "Donavan has the carriage outside, your ladyship."

"And the additional security for the house?"

"All in place."

"Good. I've asked the twins to keep watch on the streets outside. I do not expect any trouble to trail me home but I want every possibility covered."

Quinn took every instruction in stride. In her service, she suspected the man had seen more than most butlers in London. She squared her shoulders and walked from the house and down the steps to the carriage.

*Let the games begin.*


MILBANK'S WAS a unique pageant without equal in the London season. The costumes dazzled in variety but also in the vast show of wealth and glittering themes. Serena handed over her wrap to the waiting footman and then spotted no less than three Greek gods, two mermaids and one bold guest who had decided to dress the part of dragon complete with wings and a long tail that snaked behind him.

Serena was a vision of understated elegance in comparison and she was glad of it. Tonight was not the night to get lost in the crowd and in a sea of colors, the purity of her choice held a magic of its own.

She spied one or two ladies in the Black Rose and took heart. Then she spotted Harriet and had to stop herself from crying out in surprise. The Widow of Stone had transformed into an English Rose. In a dress of deepest pink with an underskirt of green silk embroidered like leaves, Harriet was a blushing flower and as pretty as any woman in the room. Her blonde hair was studded with pink sapphires and diamonds like dew and even her gloves were dyed to a pink to match. Perhaps she was the loveliest of ladies, as the change stirred reaction from everyone she passed.

"Harriet! You are wearing *pink*!"

"And why not?" Lady Lylesforth bristled defensively. "It is a costume ball, Lady Wellcott and one is encouraged to...be different than the every day."

"You can be any version of yourself that you choose to be, dearest."

"So you keep telling me." Harriet reached up to touch her hair. "Is it possible that this version of myself could now go home?"

"No. After dearest."

"After what exactly?"

Serena looked up to realize that Sir Adam Tillman and Lord Trent were heading toward them. Adam had forgone a costume and wore the finest evening clothes, his only nod to the eccentricities of their host being a simple black mask. The earl on the other hand, wore a red velvet opera coat studded with red sequins and beads, with two painted red horns poking out from his hair.

The Earl of Trent was Lucifer for the evening and Serena had to swallow hard at the hysterical bubble that rose up in her throat. *Pepper will never believe me when I tell her...*

"Lady Wellcott," Geoffrey greeted her first, making a bow with a huge theatrical flourish of his coat. "You have brought out the devil in me!"

Adam shook his head behind him and Serena wondered how many hellish puns he'd endured already. "Hardly an accomplishment I should boast of," Serena teased then smiled at Adam. "Sir Tillman. May I introduce you to my dear friend, Lady Harriet Lylesforth? Harriet, this is Sir Adam Tillman."

Adam began to take Harriet's hand when Lord Trent scoffed, "Do my eyes deceive me or has the Widow of Stone decided to play the part of a fallen flower?"

Adam froze at his uncle's affront and Harriet's gasp of fury was unmistakable. "I wonder what is sadder, Lord Trent? The notion that your rudeness no longer surprises or that you neglected to choose a donkey's ears and tail for your ensemble to more appropriately match the fact that you are a *jackass!*"

Before Geoffrey could compose a reply, Harriet lifted her hand to reveal a folded fan. "I neglected to break your nose last time, your lordship, but I'm sure I can do better!"

Serena laughed as Geoffrey's face turned a shade of red only a degree or two lighter than his coat.

"W-would you like to dance, Sir Tillman?" Harriet asked, then pressed her fingertips to her own lips, surprised at her own cheek. "It will spare me from my very first public brawl…and I would be very grateful."

Adam smiled. "I'm happy to oblige and may I say, you may have no greater admirer than myself, Lady Lylesforth, though I did mistakenly expect…someone a great deal older from my uncle's intimidated descriptions of Lady Wellcott's indomitable friend." He raked a hand through his hair, "But any woman who can set the devil on his heels and look so beautiful doing it—it is a feat."

Harriet blushed, but took his arm. "The feat is in *not* kicking him in the shins. Shall we?"

Adam made a subtle glance at Serena, hesitant to leave her alone in Trent's company but Serena smiled and waved off the pair. "Go! His lordship will need a few minutes to recover so you may safely waltz before the next round."

Adam escorted Harriet toward the ballroom, and Serena admired the sight of them together. *Perhaps there will be a slice of happiness taken from the night…for them both.*

"God, what a harridan! Serves him right if he comes off that dance floor with a black eye to show for that ridiculous act of chivalry," Geoffrey growled.

"Why do you provoke her like that? What could it possibly gain you?" she asked.

"I don't know. Women like that with their noses in their air, wound so tightly in propriety for propriety's sake that they can scarcely breathe—they defy a man to make a mistake to prove them-selves superior." His forehead gleamed with a sheen of perspiration and his words tumbled out faster and faster. "You could read their thoughts if they had any! Shallow creatures who sniff and sniff but what else can they do?"

As he went on and on, Serena tipped her head to one side, watching his anger gain momentum into a tirade without purpose. He spoke of abstracts, of the judgment of women he had never actually met and grossly condemned them all to grisly ends for imaginary insults he'd never suffered.

When she was fifteen, it was this kind of rant that would have driven her to hide in her room. At twenty-five, he looked as frightening as a child stomping his feet and throwing a useless fit.

She sighed and looked away, openly expressing her disinterest and disapproval of his conversation. She was rewarded with the distant sight of Phillip across the crowded ballroom. Like Adam, he had foregone an elaborate costume for the night, instead wearing a simple green mask to blend in to the throng. He flashed her a quick grin, an encouraging look that defied her fears. He was not hurtling himself toward her in a jealous or protective fit. He was simply there for her, just as he'd promised.

*Here for me.*

*Please God. Let him not be punished for it.*

"Lady Wellcott?"

She turned back to Geoffrey. "I'm sorry, Lord Trent. What were you saying?"

"I was saying that I am sorry for spoiling what should have been a playful and light beginning to our night."

"You are the master of games and play though I marvel that I am the only one to see it."

"Come now, you of all people know that the best games are the ones we play out of sight and where none can see. Or even better, the gambit that others can see but not believe." Geoffrey held a hand out to her. "Would you care to dance with me, Lady Wellcott?"

She nodded her assent, lightly taking his arm.

"You are not as good at hiding your cards as you think," he said. Trent leaned over to whisper as they moved toward the dance floor, "I heard a rumor recently. A snippet of gossip that made my heart stop, Lady Wellcott."

"Did you? What was it?"

"I was led to believe that you told someone else that you had hopes of a marriage—indeed that you aspired to be a *countess*."

"People talk too much."

"It was too good a secret to keep. Adam will be devastated when he learns of it but that's to be expected."

She looked at him in surprise. "He is your nephew, Lord Trent. Do not wish him ill."

"I wish him nothing but now you will dance with me, Lady Wellcott." He pulled her into the dance, breaking into the pattern without waiting for the next tune and certainly without a single thought to the awkward disruption to the dancers already enjoying their promenades. He hauled her against him and began their turns, his expression one of complete triumph. "I don't care how the boy fares!"

She gave an apologetic look to several couples over his shoulder but allowed him to lead her in the dance. "So bold, sir!"

"I cannot stop thinking about you, Serena. Not after...that was a wicked little game you were playing, to flirt so outrageously and leave me dangling like a schoolboy in the rain. Though I was hardly dangling, was I?"

"Lower your voice, Trent. Flirting was one of the skills you insisted that a lady of quality should possess. You cannot complain of it now." Serena found that it was all she could do to stay on her feet as his movements became more and more manic. She'd thought of the hours ahead, of the game's moves and countermoves, but this—this was like trying to saddle a horse in full gallop. Lord Trent needed no spur to move ahead.

"True! What a fool I would be to fuss over perfection!" He laughed. "God, what a pair we make!"

"A pair?" She smiled up at him. "A pair of what do you suppose?"

"Enough of these coy looks, woman. You made your desires clear enough yesterday and then sent me away to cool my heels. I spoke to your father at Sudbury's last week and he made it equally obvious that he wishes to see you happy. As you said, you do nothing in half measures, so I have paved the way."

"You spoke to Northland? On what topic *exactly*?"

"We will craft a future together that will shake the foundations of this world!"

"Will we?"

"What say you? A summer wedding? Shall we spend our honeymoon at Oakwell Manor and rechristen our lives with your return to your rightful place at my table?"

She deliberately stopped dancing, sending small ripples of unrest through the room as her sudden halt completely disrupted the steps of graceful couples around them. The earl's expression grew anxious and a bit impatient.

"Lady Wellcott? Are you unwell?"

"You wish to *marry* me?" she asked in open astonishment, loudly enough to gain an immediate audience of rapt eavesdropping dancers.

"Yes. As I said," he spoke, his confidence reasserting itself. "It is your joy that has overwhelmed you into this clumsy stop. Understandable, of course!" He glanced around at his peers. "I apologize. The lady was overcome."

"Your lordship," she said, then leaned in to whisper in his ear, words that only he could hear. "I am overcome at this unexpected lapse in your intellect. If I am to be Countess, why would I ever need to marry some wrinkled little bag of a man with a fraction of his vitality left to him when I can marry the young and handsome heir to that self-same estate and title and enjoy *all* that a marriage bed has to offer?"

He stiffened and began to pull away but she subtly kept hold. "Am I not all that you wanted in a woman? Is it not you who taught me that vanity was to a woman's credit and would not Adam look prettier on my arm when I am the lady presiding over Oakwell?"

She let go of him and stepped back, her face an innocent guise of anxious horror, just as the orchestra began to falter as the scene playing out on the dance floor took over the room. "I am so sorry to disappoint you—and so publicly but you've pressed for an immediate answer and...I cannot marry a man I have long seen only as a dear uncle."

"You, bitch! You godless little icy bitch!" His eyes glittered with malice as he roared in fury. The music came to a grinding and awkward stop and the entire party turned to watch the show. "I made you! I own you! You are my creature! Do you hear me?"

Serena pressed her fingertips against her lips. "I don't...understand. I was your ward but...I did not think it implied...ownership."

"You will never preside as countess over what is mine! I'll murder you both before I allow it!"

"I...my prayers did not...I would *never* have aspired to...such a thing!" Serena shook her head slowly. "You should not give rumors credence, your lordship! I have no designs to marry *anyone* and Sir Tillman well knows my choice."

"You are garbage! I plucked you out of that orphanage and made you what you are! I fed and clothed you and provided a roof over your head and saw that you had more education that any of these slack-jawed apes! And for what?"

Gasps and cries of protest ringed the ballroom, and Serena faced him undaunted. "I have learned that it was at my father's request that you took me into your house. I am grateful for your Christian care, Lord Trent." She lifted her chin a defiant inch. "I was not aware that the gift came at so high a price or I would have gladly starved to death."

"Lady Wellcott," one of the men stepped forward to offer her his arm. "Come away. The earl has forgotten himself in his disappointment."

"Yes, the poor man!" she said and gave the earl a look of open pity. "I am so sorry, Lord Trent."

"I've forgotten *nothing*!" The earl raged, striking the man's arm away from her to seize Serena's upper arm in a cruel hold yanking her back against his chest. "Don't touch her! She has fooled you all with her ridiculous charities, pious displays and the title her father secured her! She plays the lady well, doesn't she? But she is nothing! Nothing! Do you hear me?"

Serena closed her eyes as if in shame stumbling against him to whisper, "To see you braying to marry garbage and a whore...what would Warrick say?"

Gasps were the last warning she had before a cursing Trent launched himself at her. Serena tried to hold him off but his hands had seized her throat in a relentless vise fueled by raw fury and loathing as he drove her to the floor, his knee pinning her down in a ruthless assault. She struggled unable to scream as her plan yielded success she had never dreamt of. A torrent of vile hateful speech ripped out across the room, his claims so outrageous, so poisoned, that no matter what elements of truth they may have held, it was all lost.

"Bitch! Die a whore then! Die with nothing! Die and know you did not get the better of me! You did not win! I win! I *always* win!"

His audience heard only a madman and reacted slowly to save poor innocent Lady Wellcott as the surreal tone of it all held them in place. The Earl of Trent was going to murder a woman in front of them because she had refused him. It was like something out of a penny dreadful but disbelief and shock froze them in a tableau for a few critical seconds until the tide turned. Only Phillip and Adam were in motion from the start—but each man fighting against distance and the crowd to reach the earl and save her.

Her skull met with the floor and she marveled at the pain. Black sparks swam into her vision as she fought for air, unaware of the melee above her, the shouting of so many voices chiming in all at once. Women were screaming, men were yelling and the tenor of all of it was a symphony of a wolf-pack baying for the earl's blood.

It was chaos.

It was perfection.

If he killed her, he was destroyed.

If she survived it, he was destroyed.

She lost consciousness, the sparks yielding to an airless darkness that felt like black velvet pouring up through her skin.

*Imagine that. So strange...*

*Dying happens inside of you first and then the world sees it later.*

# CHAPTER 24

"There you are."

Serena opened her eyes slowly, the light from the candles making her wince but then that pain was overtaken by the agony of swallowing. She reached up to touch her bruised throat, acknowledging that no matter what she'd accomplished or expected, Serena had failed to anticipate how miserable it might be to survive.

She looked up at the relief in Phillip's eyes and raw adoration, a balm to her spirits. "I take it," she whispered roughly, "Lord Trent was not pleased to be refused?"

"Apparently no man in the history of the world has been known to have taken it worse," Phillip said.

"He does hate to lose." Serena tried to sit up, then realized that she was wearing her nightgown and that they were in her bedroom. She barely recognized her own voice, it was so raspy and rough. "H-how much time? How much time did I lose?"

"A full night and day," he supplied. "It's evening again, dearest. The doctor gave you medicine to help you sleep and for the pain. I thought Trent had cracked your skull open."

"He did not? Are you sure?" she croaked, the pain in her head so sharp she feared she would vomit.

"Your hair combs. He drove them into your scalp. Dr. West had to give you stitches but he said the scars will be completely hidden by your lovely head of hair."

"Ah, the advantages of fashion."

Phillip rearranged the pillows, adding a few to allow her to recline, settling her in with firm but gentle hands. "Rest. Mrs. Holly is in fits to send up food, your entire staff are prowling through the house on eggshells and Pepper... She has wept until she's made herself ill."

"Poor Pepper!" Serena reached up to tentatively touch her throat. "Give me a few minutes and I'll—dress and tend to her myself."

Phillip smiled and sat on the edge of the bed. "You are commanded to stay abed for at least another two days. The doctor was adamant and went so far as to recommend the locking of doors if you proved too difficult."

"I hate doctors." It was a petulant protest and Serena winced again as her voice cracked at the effort. "The only locked door will be the one he encounters when he returns."

"I'm afraid you've relinquished command until those bruises heal," Phillip said, sadly shaking his head. "Your throat looks... You are a terrifying sight, woman."

Vanity nipped at her and Serena lifted the lace collar of her gown to shield her skin from his view, glad there was no mirror handy. "Bruises heal. But what of Trent? How does it stand with the earl?"

"You'll hear soon enough. He's finished."

"It's over then." She pressed her fingers to her cheeks. "I can't believe it's finally over."

"Is it?" Phillip asked. "So easily?"

"If he is finished then that is all, Phillip." She looked away from him, proud and independent. "Do not mistake this for some spiritual quest for healing, sir. Do not think that I took Trent down to close a mystic door on my past or to put all my torments to rest. Did I take satisfaction in it? Did a part of me rejoice if I made that man kneel crying in a puddle of his own bile?" She smiled as sweetly as a child at Christmas. "There's no denying it!"

"You are terrifying. You realize this, yes?"

Serena laughed then winced at the physical toll on her throat. "What? Is honesty such a terrible virtue? I'm simply saying that I will go on. I have no false expectations, Phillip. There was no rainbow colored flash of light, no grand epiphany that will now guide me to mercy. I will still be just as I am."

"I see."

"Do you?"

He nodded. "I see that you think yourself inviolate and unchanging but we both know there's a touch of an illusion there. Every experience takes its toll, Raven. God, are we both not living examples of that —of the scars that betray our leisurely stroll along the battlefield?"

"I'm not a fool, Phillip. I have absorbed every new lesson I could and incorporated them as best I could. Have I changed? Naturally. But I want to make it clear that there is no finish line in this race, no trophy or scalp I will hold aloft and proclaim victory to retire to a shaded cabana. I don't know what happens now that Trent is destroyed, but I know that I will not be transformed into the angelic pretense of Victorian womanhood. So long as we are clear."

"Clear." His expression was solemn but she couldn't read him well enough to determine if there was disappointment in his eyes. Instead Phillip demonstrated that there was no room left for judgment between them.

He kissed her, slowly and tenderly, carefully seeking to heal what he could and to savor her presence. "Tillman is waiting downstairs. He's been here all day and refused to leave until he saw you." Phillip reached out to hold her hand. "I suspect you should hear it all from him but also that it may do you both some good to—talk."

"I'm sorry for you to meet Sir Tillman this way."

Phillip smiled. "Yes, well…He is a good man."

"Aren't you glad that the earl didn't kill him?"

"I'm not ready to jest about this, Raven. All those promises to protect yourself and you deliberately did the opposite and put yourself in harm's way. I'm so angry I can't give it words but we'll save that fight for the day when you are on your feet."

Serena crossed her arms defensively. "I only promised not to die, so pout all you want, it appears that I have yet to fail to keep *my* word. I who have generously forgiven you your faults, Warrick! So mind your toes if you think to—"

He pulled her against him, trapping her crossed arms easily to prevent the slightest resistance and kissed her into quiet. It was a tender assault that settled both their nerves but also reignited the fires between them.

"Heal, Raven." He sighed. "Fuss later. You have Tillman to reassure and I must go below stairs and tell them that their mistress has already shown signs of—remarkable recovery."

She nodded. "Yes. I will…speak to Adam."

Phillip let her go, then brought her a wrap before withdrawing. It was clear he wasn't completely pleased for her to entertain his rival in her bedroom in any state of undress but under the circumstances, it couldn't be helped.

Within minutes, a knock on the door heralded Adam's arrival and he came in, his steps uncertain as he approached her.

"Dear God. You…I can't believe he nearly murdered you in front of me."

"I'll confess I was also a little astonished," she whispered. "Sir Tillman. I owe you an apology. Your warnings were—well timed. I take full responsibility for what happened."

Adam shook his head. "You can't. I thought him obsessed but I didn't anticipate the worst. A smarter man would have seen it and not left it to you to dissuade him."

Serena waved away the notion with one hand, elegantly dismissing it. "Please. Tell me what damage has been done. Is my reputation in tatters? I'm sure Lord Trent has been trumpeting his twisted views of my refusal all over London."

She held her breath. In truth, she had no fear since whatever Geoffrey said it would be deemed meaningless. Naturally, she instead expected he'd been hauled off by the authorities for the assault, but there was no guarantees that the law's punishments would match the brutality of the Ton's. *At last, he is socially ruined—and hopefully ostracized into a lifetime of exile.*

"Lady Wellcott." Adam shifted cautiously on his feet, a man wary of speaking. "He has said nothing."

"Nothing?" Serena touched her throat reflexively.

"He was struck down by some fit after. There on the floor just as Warrick and I reached you both, he fell and began foaming at the mouth, seized by spasms the like of which I have never seen. It was chaos and by the time physicians were summoned..."

"Is he dead?" It was all she could do to pray that the wicked hope her words held would not reach his ears.

"No. Not dead. That mercy is yet denied him, Lady Wellcott. Uncle Geoffrey suffered a paralyzing stroke. He is rendered a prisoner in his own body. The doctors cannot say if he still possesses his faculties but I fear that he does."

"Is there no recovery?"

"No. They think not." Adam squared his shoulders. "The solicitors have begun the legal process that transfers his holdings and title. I am...the Earl of Trent."

There was nothing but solemn regret in his voice and Serena sympathized with a man who had never clung to ambitions of a title but who would now be forced to carry the responsibilities and burdens of one. "You will make a lovely lord, Sir Tillman. And perhaps you can teach your peers how to button their own coats?"

She was rewarded with the ghost of a smile. "At the very least."

Serena smiled back at him. "It is all unexpected but I should know that by now. Life has never gone along the course I plan for it."

"Warrick. Loves you beyond reason, doesn't he?" Adam asked softly.

Serena nodded. "In the best way a man can love, yes. He does. As I love him."

"Then I am happy for you. For you both." Adam cleared his throat and put his hands behind his back. "I am leaving London as soon as nurses can be hired and Oakwell Manor prepared for Uncle Geoffrey's return. I'll manage the estates until the legalities are finalized."

"You'll take him home?" she asked. *How beautifully perfect that Trent can be propped up in a corner to watch everything that he has and everything that he loves be managed and held in the hands of another, younger and worthier man!*

*I lose my touch that I didn't think to aim for it myself...*

"I'll take him home and reside in the dowager's cottage for my own comfort and sanity. " Adam stepped forward to take her hand, placing a warm and gentle kiss against her palm. "Good-bye, Lady Wellcott. I do hope that when you've healed, that you can recall some events of the Season with fondness."

"We are friends, still, Sir Tillman. And trust me when I say that this Season in London is one that I will never try to forget."

"You are sure?" he asked, his voice tinged with surprise.

"Oh, I am very, *very* sure."

*FINIS*

# EPILOGUE

"*L*ady Wellcott, I cannot fathom how you can help me but an old friend assures me that you are the salvation I am seeking on my sister's behalf."

Serena held up the letter she'd received from one of the Black Rose's members referring the elegant and distraught Mrs. Cavendish to her doorstep. "I have Lady Osterley's praise of your devotion to your family and of your character. She hints at some unforeseen tragedy that only I can avert but it falls to you, Mrs. Cavendish to fill in the details. Tea?"

"Oh, yes. Thank you."

Serena smiled and once again, made the tea to suit herself aware that Mrs. Cavendish wouldn't even taste the brew, that the woman was sitting in exactly the same chair that nearly all her petitioners chose to take, and that this play was oddly familiar and comforting.

"My sister. My younger sister, Mary, has only been married for a year but..."

"Go on. You could not be in a safer or more discreet place for such a conversation. Tell me the worst."

Mrs. Cavendish took a deep breath and plunged ahead. "She wrote to me that her husband had threatened to have her committed! She said he had been cold to her from the start and now had sworn to see her locked away as a hysteric and a madwoman!"

"How horrible!"

"Mary may be many things—spoiled, lively, and impulsive but she is not imbalanced, I can assure you. Even so, her claims were so shocking I could barely credit them and wondered if there could be any other explanation!"

"But now he's done it," Serena supplied.

"He's done it! I heard nothing more from her and when I inquired to him directly, he sent a brief and horrible note explaining that Mary had gone mad and he'd been forced to put her away for treatment and for her own safety! Can you imagine such a thing?" Mrs. Cavendish's face became mottled with red splotches of distress. "I was...I am much older and confess that I was always jealous of my baby sister and her beauty. I—haven't always been kind. But she reached out to me in desperation and I must trust my instincts. He is her husband and has legal authority over her. He has refused to allow us to visit her! To retrieve her! And now I fear for her life... Oh, God! My poor Mary!"

Mrs. Cavendish lost the battle to tears and Serena immediately gave her a handkerchief from her skirt pocket.

"I'm going to pace as I speak, so do not think our session over, dear lady." Serena stood to walk. "Was there a substantial dowry?"

"Vast! My father left us each a generous portion although I was far too old to apply it to securing a good match. Desmond was so charming, and although I never liked him, I was hardly in the mood to object to their marriage."

"He married her for the money and has no use for a wife. By putting her away rather than ending the marriage in divorce, he retains control of the fortune. If she dies in some hellish mental institution, then all the better from his perspective."

"He is a villain. Of that, I have no doubt, Lady Wellcott."

"Yes, but I will find out why he would move so aggressively and I will rescue your sister from her prison and from her marriage." Serena laid out the terms of the Black Rose and Mrs. Cavendish accepted them without hesitation.

Their business concluded quickly and Mrs. Cavendish left with a gleam of stern satisfaction and hope in her eyes. Serena closed the door behind her and crossed to the bell pull expecting Quinn to answer, but it was Phillip Warrick who came through the doorway from the library.

"Well?"

"I am going to Scotland. I have to rescue a damsel in distress."

He shook his head. "No."

"No?" She crossed her arms. "What do you mean *no?*"

"*We* are going to Scotland, my love. My dangerous and incomparable love."

"We. Yes. We are going to Scotland."

And the Black Rose goes on...

# ACKNOWLEDGMENTS

This is it. I think I could sneak in a paragraph about the cats since I'm really not sure anyone is reading this. But let's face it. Acknowledgements are pretty much here for the author to slip in those thank-you's that might be omitted in the rush of time, to carve them into the page so that later when your friends say, "You never named a character after me!" Then you get to counter with, "Yes, but I did say some nice things about you in the acknowledgements, remember?" (Which they naturally don't remember because who reads the acknowledgments when there's a good story in your hands that you're anxious to dive into?)

I don't blame them. But here goes. I want to thank my widening and ever more fabulous inner circle. I want to thank my Street Team, Bernard's Bombshells, for all that they do to go above and beyond for me. They say it takes a village but apparently what it really takes is a small group of dedicated ladies who will stop at nothing to achieve their goals. These are the women you want in your foxhole. Trust me.

I want to thank Lindsey Ross for keeping me sane. And Sandra Owens for sharing her with me. It's a good custody arrangement and I know that no matter what, she knows she is loved. So that's good. But meeting you in person, Ms. Owens, for the record, was one of the highlights of my journey as a writer. The biggest surprise was one of my own silly making because I truly thought that someone with such a huge talent just had to be taller. (Shows what I know.)

I'm going to have to thank Lisa Watson. Not just for making me laugh over the world's most expensive lemonade but for making my life better—simply better for knowing her.

I have to thank my husband and my daughters. One day, guys, I'll make it up to you.

I want to thank my Mom for her time, her support and mostly for teaching my daughters what it is to be loved unconditionally. (Even when those little scamps have picked almost every flower in your garden to make magical potions, redecorated your home in ways you never imagined possible and when those decibel levels hit critical on rainy days.) Wow.

And last but not least, thank you readers. For sticking with me, for your support and notes, emails and messages. And God bless you, for all those reviews! At the end of it all, the Black Rose was for you.


RB

# ALSO BY RENEE BERNARD

*The Jaded Gentlemen Titles by Renee Bernard*
REVENGE WEARS RUBIES
SEDUCTION WEARS SAPPHIRES
ECSTASY WEARS EMERALDS
PASSION WEARS PEARLS
OBSESSION WEARS OPALS
DESIRE WEARS DIAMONDS


*The Black Rose Trilogy*
LADY FALLS
LADY RISES
LADY TRIUMPHS


*The Mistress Trilogy by Renee Bernard*
A LADY'S PLEASURE
MADAME'S DECEPTION
A ROGUE'S GAME


BLIND APHRODITE


*Writing as A.R. Crimson*
BEAUTY AND THE BUCCANEER

*Contemporary Romantic Comedy Series – The Eternity Gambit*
DEVIL TO PAY
DEVIL MAY CARE


*Comic book from a story from The Eternity Gambit*
AZRAEL'S GIRL


\*\*

www.reneebernardauthor.com
www.facebook.com/ReneeBernardAuthor
Twitter - @ReneeBernard
www.historicalromanceretreat.com
www.eternitygambit.com
www.arcrimson.com

Made in United States
Orlando, FL
03 June 2022

18463391R00126